Warm sleepy mornings, waking up next
  to you
Lying real close to my side
Nothing on earth will ever come close
To the feeling I feel deep inside.

Yes sometimes it seems
You're still here with me
And maybe you're not really gone
'And one day I know we'll meet again
'Cause I have a dream that goes on . . .

'And if ever I see you again,
Maybe this time it will work out all right
Maybe this time we won't say good-bye,
But only good night
With a love that won't end
If ever I see you again.

—from the song,
   If Ever I See You Again

COLUMBIA PICTURES
PRESENTS

If Ever
I See You
Again

Starring
JOE BROOKS

SHELLEY HACK

JIMMY BRESLIN

JERRY KELLER

KENNY KAREN

Featuring
GEORGE PLIMPTON

Music composed, arranged
and conducted by
JOE BROOKS

Director of Photography
ADAM HOLENDER

Associate Producer
EDWIN MORGAN

Written by
JOE BROOKS and MARTIN DAVIDSON

Produced and Directed by
JOE BROOKS

COLOR BY TECHNICOLOR®

If Ever I See You Again

BY KERRY STEWART

BASED ON THE SCREENPLAY BY JOE BROOKS AND MARTIN DAVIDSON

BANTAM BOOKS · TORONTO · NEW YORK · LONDON

IF EVER I SEE YOU AGAIN
A Bantam Book | May 1978

ISBN 0-553-12187-1

Published simultaneously in the United States and Canada

Bantam Books are published by Bantam Books, Inc. Its trade-
mark, consisting of the words "Bantam Books" and the por-
trayal of a bantam, is registered in the United States Patent
Office and in other countries. Marca Registrada. Bantam
Books, Inc., 666 Fifth Avenue, New York, New York 10019.

PRINTED IN THE UNITED STATES OF AMERICA

If Ever
I See You
Again

PRELUDE
1964

I

The snow—a predicted seventeen inches, predicted to start "no later than noon," predicted to ruin The Entire Weekend, the weekend of the Harvard football game—held itself back until 3:27, the first flakes gracing the final down; and the final touchdown—Kenny Larkin's— was run through a beaded curtain of white.

According to schedule, ritual, rite, the game was replayed at a place called Hurley's, a campus hangout, a local bar, pretentiously known for its lack of pretension, its lobster diablo, its two-dollar wine.

Jennifer Corley, her camel's hair coat still hugging her shoulders, twisted her wineglass around on the bar and realized the glass had a chip in its base; a pie-wedged cutout that ended in points. She ran her finger around the points.

"Jen? Are you *listening?*" Larkin protested.

She nodded slowly, lifting her eyes and watching him watch her, his eyebrows beetling into a frown. He was, or so she'd described him in letters, "the absolute best-looking boy in the world"—as blond as she was, with bluer eyes, and "this perfectly, classically *GOD*like build."

"You were saying that Hamilton screwed you," she said. "You deserved a B, but you got a C-plus."

"I was *saying*"—Kenny Larkin leaned back— "that I don't see why he gives grades at *all*. I mean, seeing how he knocks the competitive spirit. I mean, Jesus, the way he puts it all down —like he thinks it was un-American or something."

"He thinks it's American," Jennifer said. And instantly suffered a sting of remorse. For mildly correcting his *stupid* remark. And for feeling so guilty, she'd built him a smile.

"Oh, Jesus," he grumbled. "You know what I mean."

"I'm sorry." She nodded. "I *do* know what you mean. Really." She put her hand on his arm, and then bundled her coat more tightly around her as the front door opened and the crowd came in. A show of pennants and loden coats, a stamping of snowy boots on the floor, a lot of whistles, catcalls, and cheers; for Kenny. The hero. The Football Star. Jennifer's boyfriend. Jennifer's Own.

I am very lucky, Jennifer thought. And twisted her wineglass around on the bar.

They started drifting into D House at seven, the men with bottles of scotch in their hands, the girls with snowflakes still in their hair.

Boots were tossed in a heap in the hallway, coats were hung on an iron rack; girls disappeared up the wooden stairway to comb their perfectly sculptured hair and color their perfectly peachy lips.

Morrison chain-lit a new cigarette and watched them from his seat at the battered piano. He let out a long, smoky yawn. He was tall, with a rangy, athlete's body, though he wasn't athletic; he didn't have time. He had high cheekbones, a straight nose, light blue eyes that were almost gray, and his hair—a wiry, shaggy brown—was getting a little too shaggy now, and as soon as he picked up a buck and a half that he didn't need for a lunch or a book, he was planning on probably getting it cut.

Morrison was not a fraternity member. Morrison was "working his way through college," a rotten cliché he profoundly despised, since it carried with it a long tradition of pimply encyclopedia salesmen and earnest scholars with fraying cuffs. He prided himself on having neither—pimples nor earnestness. Morrison worked, and worked very hard, at being indifferent, mocking, and bored.

At the moment, he was working the fraternity party, the annual D House weekend blast, as he'd worked such parties for the last three years; coaxing jazz out of untuned pianos, playing backup for drunk balladeers and various Sweethearts of Sigma Chi. (Who seemed to be partial to *My Fair Lady*, having all played Lady on the high-school stage.)

They were filtering back to the living room now, and Morrison started his Ellington set ("A-Train," "Indigo," "C Jam Blues"), and they wandered around him, sipping their scotch, in smoky little groupings of fours and eights, J. Press jackets and cashmere dresses, talking about how drunk they were getting, were going to get, had gotten before.

He played "Ipanema," which everyone sang, and then took a break around eight-fifteen, walking to the crowded bar in the corner, pouring a vodka, and looking around. The house was mostly a rich boys' club, and their dates all seemed to be angular blonds. He'd never dated an angular blond, and was almost convinced that he didn't want to. Lighting a cigarette (his last in the pack), he tasted his drink and eyed a particular angular blond sitting alone on the back of a club chair, facing a window, watching the snow. Phony-poetic pose, he decided. But he found himself watching the curve of her back.

"Hey, Bobby. You playin' piano or what? I mean, that's what we pay you for—music. Right?"

He cocked his head down at Leonard Brookman, who seemed to be nursing at a small cigar. Brookman was short, burly, dark, and wearing an orange vicuna sweater that nicely cradled his budding paunch. Morrison simply narrowed his eyes.

"Christ," Brookman sputtered, "I'm only kidding."

"Yeah. But on you it doesn't look good."

Brookman decided to look very Hurt. Which also, on Brookman, didn't look good. Changing his tactics, he growled, "Screw!" and Morrison muttered, "Quick. Get Bartlett. I'm sure he'll want to make note of that line," and next thing he knew, the blond was beside him—the window-gazer, tilting her head. She was holding a practically empty glass, and clearly she'd come to the bar to fill it, not just to stand at Morrison's side, but she looked at him now and said, "What's so clever?" and Morrison shrugged. Squinting now, he looked in her eyes. They were very, very, very blue. He was hardly able to look away.

"Brookman," he said. "He's a clever fellow. . . . Brookman, tell her the thing you just said." And turning quickly, Morrison left.

Later, feeling restless again, he decided to take his break out-of-doors, and circled slowly around the frat house, getting his feet wet, kicking up snow. He was wearing a navy-surplus sweater; turtlenecked; thick; not thick enough. Morrison shivered, and heard his mother say, "Bobby, Bobby. What are you *doing?*" so he yelled, "I'm catching pneumonia, Ma!" which made some jerk walking over to E House holler, "Hey, buddy. You talkin' to *me?*"

Morrison just kept kicking up snow. He glanced up briefly to light a cigarette. The campus looked like a Rustic Dream. The grass and the pathways, covered with white, and the wooden cottages roofed with white, and feathers of smoke coming out of their chimneys. Pastoral Idyll, he thought wryly. These Are The Finest Years Of Your Life. Bull. He'd be happy when school was finished—six more months until graduation—and then he could finally do what he wanted, have what he wanted, be what he liked . . . if he could manage to figure out what the hell it was.

Shrugging, he thought of his friend Davey. He and Davey had always been close; they'd even gone to high school together, a hard-to-get-into Manhattan school, dedicated, like the cornerstone said:

To A Higher Education In
MUSIC
AND
ART

They'd both had the same identical training. In Theory; in Practice; in Composition. They both had a feeling for Mozart, and Brahms, and hands that could make that octave-plus-two; only Davey knew what he wanted to do with it—concert piano; that was his life. And Morrison? Morrison kicked some more snow. He wasn't sure of a goddamn thing. Except that he was tired. Wrung-out. Worn. From the rotten alarm clock screaming at five, so he could get all his studying done in the morning, to free up his evenings for working at clubs—or weddings, bar mitzvahs, fraternity blasts. (Pastoral Idyll; Crock-and-a-half.) He scooped some snow from the hood of a car, packed it to a ball, and hurled it through the air in an Oscar-winning walk-on as Sandy Koufax.

Someone yelled, "Strike!"

Morrison turned. The blond was standing on the D House porch. "Aren't you *freezing?*" she said to him now. She was all bundled up in a camel's hair coat, a cashmere muffler around her neck.

"I was just going in," he said indifferently.

"Oh. Too bad. I was just going out."

He walked up the steps as the girl walked

down them, and he caught her, just as she started to fall, her orange tote bag hitting the ground, spilling out papers, pencils, books.

She flushed. "So much for grace under pressure."

Sophomore, he thought, Lit. 28, and bending over, picking things up, he saw some papers with JENNIFER CORLEY, LIT *28* written in purple ink on the top, and a library book: *The Hemingway Reader*. He held it for her while she tied her scarf.

"It's a fine book," he said dryly.

But she caught what he was doing, and nodded. "It's written on fine paper. With a fine cover."

He opened the book. It was long overdue, and he added quickly, "With a fine fine."

And Jennifer Corley suddenly laughed. There are laughs, and then there are heartwarming laughs, but this one he could feel start to warm up his toes. He studied her closely, taking his time.

Her hair was a thick tumble of yellow. Like a princess in some kind of children's story.

Her eyes were a wide impossible blue.

His attention wandered down to her mouth. Back to her eyes.

They were silent for a moment.

He kicked some snow.

She shivered again, and then said to him again, "Aren't you *freezing?*"

And this time he laughed. "You always think other people feel the way you do?"

"Oh." She gave it serious thought, frowning slightly with her head to the side, and then nodded, smiling. "Yeah. I guess."

They stood opposite each other, silent again.

Morrison felt reluctant to leave. "If you're *cold,*" he said, "why don't you come back in."

But she shook her head at him. "Had enough party. Besides, I have to go to the library now."

"Oh . . ." he said, shrugging. "Well . . . good-bye."

She stared at him a while and said, "Good night."

There were three other people in the library now—the kind of people who go to libraries on Saturday night. Obtusely, it pleased her to be among them.

She liked the library. The wide clean room with the big oak tables that always seemed to smell of furniture polish, and the oak-shelved walls that were colored with books, and the dozens of green glass-shaded lamps. There were times when she wished she could just skip classes, and instead of listening to show-off instructors with their little rep ties and their big-deal opinions, she'd simply sit here and read all the books.

Reading was becoming her favorite thing, a fact that had really surprised her at first, and something that really *disturbed* her mother. It wasn't, as her mother put it, "healthy" to "sit around mooning all day over books."

Mooning, for God's sake.

But maybe . . . *maybe* that's what it was. At least, she'd fallen more deeply in love with the men she'd met in the pages of books than the ones she met in the rest of the world. They were stronger and smarter and realer than life, and she could love them completely, with all of her heart—and then end it by simply closing the book.

There was no guilt. No reproach. None of those draggy scenes about *why?* or how could you do it? or what did you *mean?*

Like the dumb scene Kenny had started to-night. Just because she wouldn't go back into town. As though everything *he* did, *she* had to do; or else be convicted of High Treason.

Well, he'd get over it. Tomorrow. Or Monday.

She lit a cigarette and opened her book, but found that her mind kept wandering away, that her eye kept jumping up to the door, that her nails kept drumming lightly on the page.

She knew the reason and did not like it.

It was stupid.

Her heart made a sudden skip.

Purposely she kept her eyes on the book, because she didn't want to seem as though she'd hoped he would come, or been watching the doorway, or something like that. Besides, she wasn't sure that she'd *wanted* him to come, if you can make the distinction between wanting and hoping.

She wondered if you could. She looked at the clock on the library wall. 11:08.

Which meant that he'd come here straight from the party.

Still, he wasn't hurrying up to her now.

She turned a page in the history book.

He was up there talking to Laura Clark, a senior who worked as a library aide. Oblique-ly she studied the other girl's face. A dark-haired, dark-eyed *pleasant* face. He was whis-pering something, and Laura laughed.

Someone said, "Sssh."

She tried to read about ancient battles; twirled the ashtray; stubbed her smoke.

He was looking around. And now he was ...

no; he'd stopped at the stacks. Her eyes went down to the page and then up. He was leaning his arm on the side of the bookshelf; he was looking at books. He looked tired. She tapped a cigarette on the edge of the table, opened a matchbook that had no matches, and realized that something about him scared her—*scared* her—and the one thing she wanted most was to pick up her books now, put on her coat, and very quietly . . . slip through the floor.

She found a matchbook. *Rico's Car Lot. Over A Thousand Quality Cars. Close Cover Before . . .*

"You always come here to read matchbooks?"

She glanced at him slowly. Her eyes were blank. And Morrison rather ostentatiously shifted the books around in his hands. As though to say: Listen, I came here to *work*, so keep your eyes just as blank as you want.

She said, "You've got something on the top of your head."

He squinted. *"Huh?"*

"Sit down."

He sat. And pursing her lips, she ran her fingers down through his hair and pulled out a piece of magenta wool. He had no idea how the hell it got there. But it got him sitting at Jennifer's side, and she smiled, as though she expected him to stay. She went back to her reading.

Morrison read. Or at least he made sure that he turned the pages, and didn't watch her with the side of his eyes any more often than the law allowed. The law being Robert Morrison's Law of Self-Preservation: DO NOT WANT. That was the law. Thou shalt not covet nothin', baby, unless it's something you know you can get. And seen from a certain practical angle, Jennifer Corley was a Steinway piano, a brand-new shiny '64 car, and a million dollars in one-dollar bills.

At exactly midnight, the library closed.

He asked if she'd like to go for a pizza.

She said she would.

They stopped at his apartment to pick up the keys to his roommate's car. Turning once, on his way to the bedroom, he saw her sitting on the edge of his desk; her hair shimmered in the overhead light, and the elevator loosely attached to his heart made a quick round trip to the floor and back, and the wit of Kipling ran through his head as he searched the dresser, finding the keys.

> *A fool there was and he made his prayer*
> *(Even as you and I!)*
> *To a rag and a bone and a hank of hair*
> *(We called her the woman who did not care)*
> *But the fool he called her his lady fair—*
> *(Even as you and I!)*

They drove into town through falling snow.

She told him she came from California and until last winter she'd never seen snow. She loved it.

He said, "There's snow and there's snow," mentioning the gray, garbage-strewn heaps that sat on the sidewalk for weeks in the Bronx.

After that she was silent. And Morrison suddenly laughed out loud.

"What's funny?" she said.

He shook his head. "Nothing. Me. Romantic chap. He sings her a ballad of dirty snow."

And then to his surprise, she turned it to a game. They made up "The Ballad of Dirty Snow."

She said she was fairly sure it began "My heart leaps up when I behold a pile of graying slush . . ." and after they'd filled in a few more lines, he provided the couplet, wrapping it up: "It's a haven for garbage 'er else it's a harbinger . . . telling of romance and mush."

She said, "No. 'Of love that is lush.' "

He told her she was clearly a hopeless romantic.

He wasn't really sure how the rest of it happened.

They drank a lot of wine, but that wasn't it.

He preferred to think it was luck; or charm; or at least a more elegant chemistry than Gallo's.

She seemed to watch more than listen to him talk, and she followed all the leaps and quirks of his mind; her humor delighted him, canceled forever the wishful cliché that beautiful women had to be dumb. They shared cigarettes. Gobbled pizza. She said she'd loved it when he sang at the party, and she said he'd sounded like Gene Kelly. She made him feel he was Gene Kelly. She made him feel he could probably dance, and do a bunch of other impossible things.

They walked through the snowy, sleeping town.

She asked him what he thought he'd do after school. She meant, of course, do-for-a-living. He said he didn't know. She watched him and smiled. "Everyone I know," she said, "knows. They know they want to be a lawyer or something, and what's even worse, they've *always* known. I mean, isn't it *wonderful* not to know? It means you could be . . . anything at all. . . ." He said: "Or nothing." She said: "Oh, no."

And then they were back at his apartment again, with the record player spinning out "A Taste of Honey"; and, sitting next to him, she turned her head, so her hair was splashing all over his chest, and he cupped her chin gently in his hands, and slowly, endlessly tasted her mouth.

She let him carry her into the bedroom, and she said, "Isn't this the way Rhett carried Scarlett?" and he said, "Oh, God. Are you gonna be Scarlett?" And then, because he didn't want the answer to that, he kissed her, setting her down on the bed.

He'd never been more joyful in his life; he'd never been more completely serene. His feelings were of ease, of a powerful warmth, of a really almost-terrible tenderness. He found a sweetness in the way she clung to him. And then, when it was over, she purred in his arms, put her head on his chest, and was instantly asleep.

For an hour he lay there stroking her hair, and then realized he was very tired himself. The bedside clock said ten after four. Reluctantly Morrison let himself sleep.

When she woke, he was very faintly snoring, and the tiny bedroom was flooded with light, showing a dance of dust in the air.

The room was cold. Or anyway, she shivered. And watching his face (there were already small knifelike lines that ran like parentheses around his mouth), the only thing she felt was a flutter of fear.

She thought about leaving before he woke, leaving a note ("Disregard Last Message"), but then he was stirring, moving his arm, making a low, deep-throated grunt, and opening his eyes, which she carefully avoided.

He tested the waters, and found them troubled. He hid his face behind cigarette smoke and affected a slow, sleep-fuddled manner, trying to avoid the greater pitfalls of being either defensive or defenseless. He said he had "a lot of things to do today" but suggested they might "grab a quick breakfast."

She said okay, as long as it was quick, because she really had a lot of things to do today.

He watched her walk to the ladderback chair, pulling her sweater from under his jeans, finding her tights wrapped up in his shirt. He waited till she'd moved with her clothes to the john, and then quickly, angrily put on his own.

It was better at the diner. Davey was there with Laura Clark, and Warner, with a Lucy Something-or-other—a bundle he'd met at Rinaldo's Bookstore, a girl he'd somewhat bleakly described as "a Vassar body with a Brooklyn head." His description was right, but she seemed to be pleasant, and clearly the two of them had something on. Davey and Laura were especially close, and sitting in the booth, lighting a cigarette, Morrison started to feel like himself, if not exactly like Gene Kelly.

The coffee helped. The company helped. The

taste of bacon and eggs was reviving. But Jen was a stranger. A girl who happened to be sitting at the table. Lucy said she had to drive to the station, and Warner, the gallant, walked her to the door. Jennifer watched him, and just for a second Morrison wished he had Warner's looks—halfback body with a ski-bum face—but then he thought to hell with it and stubbed his cigarette.

Warner came back, grinning a little, and Davey pushed his empty plate to the side, put his arm around Laura, and said, "Okay. All right. We've got an announcement to make."

"Uh! Don't tell us," Warner said quickly. "Gotta let us guess." He looked from Davey to Laura and back. "Is it something disgustingly romantic?" he guessed.

Laura nodded. "Disgustingly," she said.

"A chocolate-covered Carvel Valentine Cake," Morrison suggested.

"Wait," Warner said. "Let's not just buckshot." He looked at Davey. "Is it bigger than a breadbox?"

Davey flushed. "All right, you creeps. Neither of you gets to be best man anyway. What we decided"—he took Laura's hand—"is, considering the quality of friends around here, we're gonna have a *worst* man." He turned to Morrison. "And that's you, Bob."

Morrison nodded. "I'll do my worst."

"Right." Davey grimaced. "We can count on that. Now what we're missing is a father of the bride." He looked at Warner. "So what do you think?"

"Hell, I don't know"—Warner seemed to think—"does it mean I have to rent a paternity suit?"

Everyone groaned. Warner frowned. "Not that I question the casting department, but why should *I* be the father of the bride? *Bob's* the one who's old enough to be her father."

"Yeah. But we figured he'd fight the decision. He's old enough to fight," Davey explained.

"And he was old enough to vote," Laura considered.

"For Calvin Coolidge," Morrison said, and seeing Jennifer tilt her head, he added flatly, "I'm twenty-three."

Jennifer looked at him. "Why?" she said.

He shrugged. "Because it came after twenty-two."

"I mean, why——"

"I lost a year out of school as a kid."

"He was kidnapped," Warner eagerly explained, "by a wandering band of lecherous nannies."

"Who took him, it's said, to a South Sea island, where they . . . No!" Davey stopped. "It was too awful. He developed amnesia and eventually died."

A better answer than "rheumatic fever." Also funnier.

Morrison laughed.

Charlie Williams came over to the table, bummed a cigarette from Morrison's pack, and grinning, said Morrison smoked too much, so he was only taking it for Morrison's health. Charlie Williams were premed, and his line to every girl on the campus was to ask her if she'd like to play doctor with him. He asked Jennifer. Jennifer said she'd rather play dentist, and she'd try not to hurt him when she pulled out his teeth.

Morrison gave her an appreciative laugh, and

she lent him a quick trace of a smile and then
looked at her watch and said," Oh-oh. Wow.
I really have to go."

Watching her pick up her bag and her books,
Morrison supposed he should just let her go;
should stay here with his friends, have another
cup of coffee, ask about the wedding, stay
where he belonged, but when she pulled out her
wallet he snapped, "Oh, for Christ's sake, Jen,"
and reached in his pocket, yanked out a five,
tossed it on the table, and picked up his coat.
"Come on," he said wearily. "I'll walk you."

They walked across campus, watching their
feet make tracks in the snow. He kept on wanting to put his arm around her, just pull her
close to him and say, "Where are you?"

Hands in his pockets, he said, "Where are
you?"

She said she was thinking of the work she
had to do.

He nodded, knowing he'd gotten his answer.
But he still wasn't ready to leave it alone.
They were passing what was known as Dangerous Mountain—a low and perfectly safe little
hill where people went sledding. A sled came
down; a guy was steering, and the girl, who
was double-deckered on his back, was screaming and laughing at the same time.

Morrison scooped up a handful of snow.
"Anything particular you'd like to discuss?"

"Particular?" she said, and shook her head
no.

And then he was suddenly, nastily angry.

Because he knew The Law, but he'd gone
ahead and broken it; knew the part, but he'd
gone ahead and played it. Like a clown who

signs up to slip on a banana peel, he didn't have the right to holler he'd been hurt. You asked for it, buddy. You volunteered.

And he almost felt sympathetic to her now. Poor baby. Poor Jen. Woke up this morning in a crummy bedroom in a crummy apartment with the janitor's son. Title this playlet *The Princess and the Pauper: A Comic Opera.* In One Act.

She shivered again, and he said, "California. It doesn't prepare you for rougher climes."

She said: "I'd better get a warmer coat."

He said: "I guess you'd better try for a mink."

"Sable," she said. "It's more expensive."

"Maybe you'll get one for Christmas," he said.

They continued walking, silent for a while.

"I really wouldn't want one," she said in a burst.

And he wanted to stop himself, honestly did, but he didn't. "Ah-hah. She's a pure-hearted girl. All she really wants is one perfect rose."

They were standing in the courtyard in front of her dorm. They looked at each other. He watched her eyes.

"I don't know," she said, and lowered her eyes.

He nodded curtly, turning away; and then turned back suddenly, yanked her by the arm, and kissed her harshly; then he walked away.

"Hey, Jen? There's a call for you," Caroline yelled. She was standing in the hallway holding the phone. From the lounge came the sound of the Sunday Night Movie.

Jennifer stood in the doorway of her room. "Who is it?" she mouthed.

"It's Kenny," Caroline mouthed in return. Relieved, Jennifer walked to the phone.

"You're really a jerk," Warner was saying. He opened a beer and handed it to Morrison, who sat, nodding slowly, in the middle of the floor. Davey was sitting on Morrison's desk. He ran a hand through his thinning hair, said, "Good. And now that we've got that settled, why don't we talk about something else. Like Jennifer Corley." He reached for a beer.

They'd been talking about her for the last half-hour.

Morrison even had the grace to laugh.

"What *makes* you such a jerk," Warner went on, "is not the reason you *think* you're a jerk. What makes you such a jerk is your lack of good taste." He sipped his beer now. "Listen, ol' buddy, this chick is a zip. She's a spoiled, shallow little pom-pom girl, and—"

"You're wrong about that."

"Like hell I am."

Morrison squinted at Warner for a while. Warner (Major Basketball Star, Most Likely to Succeed with Any Girl in the World) had a definite aversion to "pom-pom girls," claiming he'd dated them for seventeen years and the only thing that flowered in their heads was their hair. Morrison now took a swig of his beer and said, "You know you're a bigot? You're really a snob. I'm telling you, Warner, the girl's *got* something."

"Long blond hair, baby. That's all it is. Man. Any other guy in your position would just walk away sayin,' 'Whoopee. I scored.' "

"Wrong. Or I'm not like any other guy. And I tell you, she's not like any other girl."

"Right. That's right. You're completely unique. Never before in the history of love have we had such a pair of unusual characters. Shakespeare, in his grave, is rolling in agony, to think he had to die before he found this plot."

"Terrific. Wonderful." Morrison scowled. "I'm in major distress that you find me boring, but I'd like to point out, may the jury take note, that *I'm* not the one who opened this subject. I don't recall saying a thing."

"Right," Warner said. "Not a thing. For forty-eight hours." He turned to Davey. "You ever try rooming with a silent man? 'Good morning,' I say, and it's Black Look Time."

"What 'Good morning'?" Morrison said. "You haven't slept home in a week and a half."

"And aren't you glad."

They were silent for a while.

"Why," Davey offered in a tentative voice, "why don't you just go and talk to her, Bob?"

Morrison shrugged. "Because I know what she'll say."

"You *don't* know what you'll say. That's the whole point. And you haven't even given her a chance to say it. Maybe she's nutty in love with you, right? Maybe she's been chewing her nails by the phone."

"I doubt that strongly."

"But you don't *know*. So see her and get it over with, man. You're sittin' here playing a suspended seventh. Resolve that chord, you know what I mean?"

By the time she saw him, it was much too late. She was halfway down the stairs with her coat on her shoulders, and he saw her, and started to rise from his chair. The desk had phoned up and said, "Someone to see you," and she'd thought it was Kenny, who was taking her to town.

And still, she wasn't exactly surprised. She'd thought it was possible he'd finally come, had in fact all along vaguely expected him, but seeing him now, she wanted to run. His very presence seemed to *ask* for something. He seemed to be a kind of living *Demand*. But that wasn't it. He'd demanded nothing. On Sunday, he'd read her, and just walked away. She'd been grateful for that, liked him for that. But now he was here. Come to collect. To punish her by making her push him away.

There was nothing she could do but go to him now. Other couples were meeting in the lobby; quick kisses; the television set, showing the Tuesday six-o'clock news.

He was wearing the same old navy-blue sweater and gray flannel pants. And then when she was next to him, he offered the faintest odor of lime, and she could picture him standing at his bathroom sink, splashing his face with a lime-colored lotion, and the picture of it practically made her cry.

He shrugged now and said, "I guess I should have called. You've got a date."

She nodded.

He grinned, shrugging again. "Yeah. Well ... I thought ... uh ... maybe we should talk. Have dinner or something. So maybe tomorrow. It's just that ... uh ... I found out at the last minute that I wasn't working tonight. And I ... uh"—he paused—"don't seem to be too articulate tonight. I'll call you tomorrow. Maybe I'll ... uh ..." Morrison winced. He didn't seem able to either talk or stop talking. Her beauty was really terrible; it hummed in his eyes.

She sighed. "I guess we should talk now. Why don't we go for a walk or something."

He nodded, taking his coat from the chair. He felt like a fool. Having known he shouldn't come, he knew he should go. But then again, maybe Davey was right. He should hear the words. He held the door as she buttoned her coat, and she walked out, brushing against his chest.

The air was a very clean black. There were stars, and the moonlight glistened the snow. They walked to a small covered bridge and up to the edge of a frozen pond.

He leaned on a railing. "Shoot," he said.

She licked her lips, feeling the wind bite up against them. She hadn't known it would be this hard. *Shoot,* he'd said. And he looked like someone about to be shot. He was even smoking The Last Cigarette. But the actual *paradox* of it was that he seemed so firm in his vulnerability, so compelling in his plaintiveness. She shivered; and he smiled. And for one quick second, what she wanted to do was fall into his arms, not ever leave them, and thinking it made her shiver again, and she heard the slamming of a million doors; doors to the future, doors to the past. She shivered and said, "This is all wrong."

He watched her patiently. "What's all wrong?"

"You. Me. Us. It's wrong. I thought about it, Bob. It's just . . . not." She moved from the railing, walked to the pond.

"Why?" he asked her, following slowly. He put out a hand and touched her on the shoulder, turning her around. "I want to know why."

His voice was flat, uninflected. His eyes were very steady and calm. "I'm serious, Jen. I want to know why. I want to know if it's my looks or my character, or the way I live, or if I've got bad breath. I want to know what made you run last Sunday, almost as much as I want to know why you were there at all. I want to know if I'm the only one who felt something Saturday night. . . ." He realized how much like a fool he sounded, but he didn't really care. She'd think he was a fool whatever he said. So he said, "Because I'm probably in love with you, Jen, and I just . . . and I just want to know, that's all."

She couldn't stand it. She didn't want to be here, didn't want to do this, didn't want to make him feel any pain. People were hurt too easily, she thought. You touched them and they broke. It wasn't fair.

She said, "It's simply that there's somebody else. It's got nothing to do with you. Nothing at all."

"You're in love with him?"

"Yes," she said staunchly. "Wildly," she added, to make it stick.

He simply nodded.

"I suppose you hate me," she whispered. "I'm sorry."

He cocked his head at her, frowning. "No. Sorry," he said. "I don't hate you."

"Oh," she said.

"You'll be late for your date. Come on." He rested his hand on her arm.

On the porch, he leaned up against a railing and said: "I left you something at the desk."

"What?"

"I guess you'll have to check at the desk."

"Oh." She lowered her head for a moment. Her hair was the color of May wine. "I like you," she said. "You're . . . very nice."

"Nice," he said. "It's nice to be liked. He tossed his cigarette butt to the air, watching it die in a shower of sparks. Turning, he looked at her standing beside him, then lifted his shoulders and said, "Good-bye."

She stared at him slowly and said: "Good night."

At the lobby desk, in a cone of waxy florist's paper, she found the single yellow rose.

1977

II

A light snow was falling on Fifth Avenue, and a fast cold wind was tossing it around. Six floors down, on the darkening street, a couple of foxes in minks' clothing struggled with sharp important umbrellas and tried for a taxi from Tiffany's door. There were no taxis. And never would be, Morrison thought, and turned away from the men's-room window and back to the mirror. He rubbed his eyes. They were ringed with blue, marbled with red. A living eyedrop commercial, he thought. He lowered his glasses back to his eyes (which looked even worse when he saw them clearly) and ran his hands straight back through his hair as a hundred-eighty decibels of Acid Rock pounded on the door and, uninvited, crashed through the threshold and bounced off the tiles. The mirror rattled. Morrison moaned and, opening the door, stepped into hot, smoky chaos.

They called it a Blast.

Federal Sound Invites You To Attend Our 17th Anniversary Blast—17 Truly "Record Years" Of Serving Our Friends From Madison Ave.

They had eight trillion Friends from Madison Ave., and all of them jammed into Studio A. A for Admen; A for Effort. Morrison stood there, holding his breath, and glomming the noise, the smoke, and the crowd (thirty-dollar haircuts and seven-bill suits, the girls with their eyebrows plucked to Astonishment, smiling darkly with This Year's mouth) and simply wanted to pick up and run.

Warner yelled, "Smile."

"What?"

"Smile!" He slapped a glass into Morrison's hand, leaning over so his beard was tickling Morrison's ear, said, "Smile, baby. They're playin' your song."

The worst of it was, they were playing his song. The song he'd written for Jungle perfume. *Not* a jingle, a song. A *love* song to a two-ounce bottle of yellow that smelled just ever so slightly of Pledge, that got your man while it polished your table, removing stubborn stains from your neck, four-ninety-five in your grocer's freezer, or wherever beautiful people are sold.

Morrison stood there hating it now. You heard it on television almost constantly. Radios blared it in diners and cabs. Jungle ("Because it's a jungle out there") was a brand-new fragrance (seven weeks old) and was being in-

troduced with a media blitz known as a "satura-
tion campaign."

Which seemed to be working; just like a
charm. In the first two weeks that the product
was out, two million women had run to their
stores, and according to a feature in *TV Guide,*
the reason was probably Morrison's song.

The article (titled "Buy-Buy, Baby") was all
about Morrison Music Inc., calling its owner "The
King of the Jingle," "The Pied Piper of Madison
Ave."

Morrison (it said) had lured more women
(into drugstores, markets, and specialty shops)
than any other living man on the planet. Morrison (it said) knew "all about Eve," knew that
a girl did not give a fig leaf for GL-90 or Overhead Cam, so his commercials told her, in a sexy
voice, "can't resist you, baby," or informed her
hoarsely, when she entered the room (with her
Jungle perfume)

> *My heart beats:*
> *Dum da-da-dum*
> *Just like a*
> *Drum da-da-dum*
> *Oh here you*
> *Come da-da-dum*
> *da-da-dum*
> *I want . . .*

The band was really clobbering it now. Morrison swallowed a half-ounce of scotch. A red-
headed girl in a yellow dress was hollering
something he couldn't hear, but he smiled, nodding, and the girl laughed. An elbow hit him

smack in the ribs, and he turned, as another one hammered his spine, and an Office Blond went elbowing by with a paper plate full of cold pastrami.

He turned to Warner. "I can't take it."

"What?"

"I said, gotta *shake* this scene."

Warner shook his head. "I can't hear you."

Morrison waved a disgusted hand and, turning, started to swim for the door. You could make it, he figured, with an overhead stroke, covering easily two feet an hour, if you just kept pushing shoulders from your path and smiling Excuse Me, which no one would hear. Only he swam himself into a corner. Right near the bar. Nobody budged. Somebody shoved a glass in his hand. Somebody tripped. The music died, voices tumbled on wounded ears, and somewhere a plummy tone was intoning, ". . . and the only really *meaningful* art is the art of selling"; and someone agreed.

Morrison moved an inch and a half. Kramer Norris winked at him now. Norris was standing with the red-headed girl and another girl wearing a lime-colored dress. Norris said, "Hey, man, whaddaya say?" and Morrison nodded. "Help," he said.

The lime-colored lady bobbled her head. "Hell. You're right. It's absolute hell. The fire department could raid this place."

"They couldn't get *in* here to raid this place."

"You're cute," she said. "Do you really make two hundred thousand a year?"

"What?" He needed a drink on that, and it just so happened there was one in his hand.

The girl was giggling, lighting a cigarette. She had purple eyelids and brownish lips and a curly halo of cinnamon hair. "The Gospel According to *TV Guide.*"

"I don't know," he muttered. "I haven't read it."

"You're kidding."

"No." He wasn't kidding. Warner had read him some lines on the phone, but he hadn't seen it. He started to turn. Norris was pulling him back by the arm.

"Hey, look. Let's all do a dinner tonight. You and Rosie and Janet and me." He indicated the pair of girls.

"Uh-uh. Sorry. I gotta get home."

"You must be divorced," the redhead observed.

"I must?"

She shrugged. "This is New York City. I never met a *married* man who went home."

"Cute."

"It isn't," she said, "but it's true."

Warner was standing over by the door, and Morrison handed the redhead his drink, said, "Cry in this for me," and started to go. The one place he wanted to go was to bed. Alone. To bed (and perchance) to sleep. He hadn't been sleeping well for a week. He'd been working hard, and he'd hit the pillows, feeling he could sleep for a thousand years, and then *nothing;* he'd lie there with a head full of tunes, like a record player he couldn't turn off, and then after a while, he'd go with the tunes, start to arrange them, (cello and vibes), and after a while he'd bring in the brass, bring it in loud, and then louder than that, till it built so

loud that it drowned out the words, which were,
*What the hell are you doing, Morrison? What
the hell are you doing it FOR?*

(Two hundred thousand dollars a year.)

"Hey, Bobby."

He'd walked into Hamilton Rush. Literally,
into him, spilling his drink. Rush now smiled
as he brushed himself off. He was tall and pale
and splendidly groomed, with a headful of beau-
tifully silvered hair and a look of finely bred
stupidity. Morrison muttered apologies now.

"Think nothing of it. Nothing at all." Rush
pulled a handkerchief out of his pocket and
patted a brown cashmere lapel. "So how does it
feel to be man of the week?"

"I think Sadat is the man of the week."

"I mean your picture in *TV Guide*. You know
the issue came out today."

"So I've heard."

"Mmm. She describes you as lean and sardonic."

"Yeah. Listen, Ham. I'm kind of in a hurry.
Excuse me?"

"Sure. I'll see you tomorrow."

"*Tomorrow?*" Morrison thought: Tomorrow.
Presentation. The airline commercial. Oh,
Christ. And he hadn't even written it yet.
"Right," he said. "See you tomorrow.

"Warner, Warner," he said softly as they
walked through the door to the quieter hall.
Some Serious Drinkers sat on the floor, and a
couple was necking in the darkened control
room of Studio B. "I forgot the—"

"Airline commercial. You want me to try to
put it off for a day?"

"No. We can't. Wednesday we're doing—"

"The Buick movie. And Thursday's Thanksgiving."

Morrison squinted. "What do you mean it's Thanksgiving. It's only the seventeenth."

"I mean we're recording a hundred and twelve Thanksgiving commercials for Waldamer's Markets. Save on turkeys. Save on Waldamer's canned—"

"I got it. How about stalling Rush until Monday?"

Warner shook his head. "Not if they want to make air on time. They're pushing this California package for two weeks only, starting the first."

"Terrific. I guess it's back to the keyboard." Morrison fumbled around in his pocket till he pulled out the metal coat-check disk. He handed it up to the hatcheck girl, who looked at it briefly and turned to the coats. "I suppose you wouldn't feel like writing it for me?"

"Sorry. Tone deaf." Warner flashed him a ski-bum grin.

"Great. I should have gone into business with a writer."

"Yeah? A *writer*," Warner came back, "could never put up with a Hamilton Rush. And all the other jerks I gotta put up with. Just remember, while you sit there peacefully plunking your piano, I'll still be here making tiny little talk."

"We also serve who only stand and drink."

"Something like that."

Morrison grabbed his coat from the counter and noticed a cigarette burn on the sleeve. "Seedy," he said. "Really seedy." He looked at Warner. Warner looked Dapper. He always looked Dapper. Warner would probably still look Dapper on the morning of the twentieth day of The Flood.

Warner walked him to the elevator now. "Speaking of seedy, your housekeeper called."

Morrison frowned. "I miss the connection."

"She said you promised Amy some chrysanthemum seeds. For a school project."

"I got them."

"Oh. Man. You're really something and a half. Forget to do a great big airline commercial, but you don't forget your daughter's chrysanthemum seeds."

"You jealous?"

Warner built a wicked grin. "Nope. But I gather Caroline was."

The elevator opened. Morrison held it. "What's that supposed to mean?"

"Caroline Walters? The ravishing redhead you met at my house? my wife's very closest friend in the world? the one she was hoping you'd marry next summer so someone would help her with the dishes on the boat?"

"So?"

"You took her to lunch on Sunday."

"So?"

"You took her to lunch with your kids."

"So?"

"She didn't love it too much. Your first date, Morrison. Use a little sense."

The elevator door was fighting his hand. Morrison punched it back into line. "Listen. I don't see enough of my kids, and on Sunday I'm not gonna leave them, all right?"

"Listen," Warner said, "it's none of my business—"

"Right."

"And they're beautiful, wonderful kids. But they're ruining your love life."

"They *are* my love life."

"Spoken like a true Benedictine monk."

Sighing, Morrison nodded his head. "Don't knock it. They make a pretty good brandy."

He entered the elevator, punching the *1*.

III

There was a leather chair in his workroom at home that looked like an oversized baseball mitt. It was mitt-colored, soft, and it swiveled around, and he swiveled around in it, smoking, staring at the snow through the window, and trying to think about California.

(*"Fly there while it lasts—only 2 weeks more!"*)

Sun; sunsets; palm trees; surf.

Nothing.

And then the old joke came back. A couplet he'd written for a comedy song, a first-act closer for a show called *Blitz*—a show he'd described to the *Guide* reporter as "a really astoundingly redolent turkey that died a friendless New Haven death."

"Blond and Blue" was the name of the song.

It was sung by a disappointed would-be actress who was warning a couple of other young girls to avoid all the Terrible Errors she'd made, and among her entreaties she'd tossed:

> *And I warn ya*
> *Skip California*

It was sung by Kate.

Lest We Forget.

"Daddy?"

"What?" Morrison swiveled. Johnathan stood there, losing his pajamas, blinking in the light. "What is it, honey? It's a hundred o'clock. You ought to be deep in the billows of sleep."

"It's ten after ten," Johnathan said.

"Digital clocks," Morrison grumbled. "They're taking the fantasy out of our lives. C'mere." He buttoned Johnathan's buttons and quickly tousled the corn-colored hair. "What ails you, kiddo?"

Johnathan yawned. "Nothin'. Had to go to the pot."

"I think you're old enough to call it the can. How old are you? Twelve?"

"Six."

"Then you better call it the pot." Morrison frowned at his son's round face, trying to hide his outrageous pleasure at the sight of this tiny night visitor who grinned at him now and said, "What're ya doing?"

"Well . . . what does it look like I'm doing?"

Johnathan cased him with sleepy blue eyes. "Nothin'," he said.

"Right. And when I look like I'm doing nothin', what am I doing?"

"Working."

"Right."

"On what?"

"Columbia Airlines song, and you're sleeping on your feet. I'll walk you to bed."

They started to walk through the large apartment.

"I'm thinking of a word," Johnathan said, playing the rhyme game Morrison had taught him, "that rhymes with 'warm.'"

Morrison thought, biting his lip. "Is it what it's doing outside right now?"

Johnathan sighed. "Yeah. It's 'storm.'"

Morrison opened the bedroom door. His daughter, Amy, was sound asleep on the upper bunk. He straightened the sheets on the lower bed, and Johnathan quickly got under the covers.

"I'm thinking of a word," Morrison whispered, "that rhymes with 'Columbia.'"

Johnathan thought. "I don't know."

"You don't know? Well, that's pretty dumbaya."

Johnathan giggled. "You're silly, Daddy."

"You're darn right. When I stop being silly, you better shoot me."

"You're silly."

"Good night," Morrison whispered, and kissed the top of his son's head.

At the doorway he paused and looked back for a moment. Amy rolled over, facing the wall. Johnathan was probably nearly asleep. The pie-shaped wedge of light from the hall lit on the yellow light of his hair.

Kate's hair.

Lest We Forget. . . .

It was early October. Sixty-seven. It was raining, sleeting, icy cold. They'd been in New

Haven for over a week; the show was in terrible terminal pain.

Kowalsky, the hotshot Brilliant Director, was very obviously going insane, *criminally* insane, Morrison had said, because he'd taken a funny, bright little tale about actors in Hollywood during the Depression and was molding it into *Tobacco Road*. Or, as somebody said, "My God. He's making the Depression depressing."

That, in itself, was bad enough. Worse was that Morrison had to keep writing—throwing out good songs and putting in bad ones, or songs that at least kept turning out bad because he hated the thought of them. And then, even *worse* . . .

He stopped turning out songs. One day they just stopped coming at all. Nothing came to his mind; nothing came to his hands. It didn't get better the second day, either. He sat at the piano playing "Pop Goes the Weasel." The third day Kowalsky dunned him for a song, and Morrison told him, "Relax, I've got it," and started playing "Begin the Beguine." It wasn't funny. He was dying inside. But one of the talents he'd lately acquired was the talent of grinding pain into jokes. Desperate men are desperately funny. And what was more desperate than being a writer who couldn't write? a composer without a tune in his brain? On the fourth day, he waited around to be fired. But then, to his surprise, the director was fired, and the new director said: "Write a comedy song."

Nothing.

He remained stuck.

Completely stuck.

Stuck in a diner at a quarter of three, drinking lukewarm, day-old, pitch-black coffee, trying crazily to keep himself awake so he could think of . . .

Nothing.

The girl walked in with another dancer. She was looking tired and wistfully Down. Of course, he'd seen her before in the chorus; "picked her out of the chorus line." She was pretty, a blond, and not very tall, and she nodded hello, and then sat in a booth at Morrison's left, two aisles over. He ordered more coffee and watched her idly, liking (of all things) the set of her chin (it was square, and it had a determined little jut), and the only thing he really overheard from his booth was her saying, "So listen, I warn you, just *don't*. . . . and for God's sake, *never* . . ." And he got the idea for "Blond and Blue."

It was one of those songs that simply *happened*, was born, full-grown, in the back of his brain, and then knocked on his head and said, "Hey, let me out." It started to write itself out on a napkin, and he'd raced from the diner, clutching the thing, and run to his hotel room, where it sang itself to him.

And then he went nuts. Totally nuts. At five in the morning, exhausted, elated, unshaven, absurd, he'd grabbed up the newly completed lead sheet and banged on the lady's hotel-room door.

(She said to him later: "What would have happened if I hadn't been alone?" He said: "Look. Nothing happened and you *were* alone.")

What happened was that he gave her the song.

"To *do*," he said. "I want you to do it."

"Onstage?"

"In the bathtub. Of *course* onstage."

She tilted her small, curly blond head. "I think the director assigns the numbers."

Of course the director assigns the numbers, but Morrison fought for a day and a half, and she finally got it.

And took him to bed.

In the dark New Haven hotel room—his—with the wastepaper basket full of coffee containers and the seventeen million cigarette butts, she lay down beside him with her taut little body and he heard himself saying, "Hey, listen, kiddo, you're supposed to sleep with me to *get* the part, not after you've got it," and, "Listen, baby, I don't wanna mislead you, they'll probably cut it in rehearsal tomorrow," and he kept rambling on like that, and she said, "My heavens, I thought you were the strong, silent type," and he said, "Wrong movie. I'm weak and verbal," and she said, "Shut up."

They were married in March.

In May, after months of looking for work, she burst through the doors of their West Side apartment and burbled: "I just got a part in *Hair*."

He nodded slowly. "Is it in the middle?"

"What?" she said.

"The part in *Hair*."

"Yuch!" she said, but she laughed and kissed him, and lifting her up, he whirled her around, and they celebrated with drinks at Sardi's and a night of exuberant candlelit sex.

By June she was pregnant.

"The rabbit died."

"One less rabbit, one more kid. A fair exchange." Morrison grinned.

"It isn't funny." She snapped, "It means I'll have to give up the show."

"There'll be others," he said.

But it didn't work. *This* was the role that would ride her to fame, and her hatred of Morrison grew with her stomach. As though he had done something quite spiteful.

"I'm a house," she said at the bedroom mirror. *"House?* My God, I'm a damn hotel."

"A grand hotel," he tried, "it's grand," and he tried to put his hand on her stomach.

"Oh, shut up, will you? Leave me alone."

Given no choice, he left her alone.

He started to write an industrial song for Buick. "A Broadway musical," he explained to Davey. "Only, instead of Boy Meets Girl, the theme of this one is Boy Meets Car."

It was dumb, but it earned him eight thousand dollars. He bought her a diamond clip. She liked it. For almost a night she was nice.

When Amy arrived, to Morrison's surprise, and despite all the Blighted Career complaints, Kate wasn't eager to rush back to work. She'd discovered, he found, in the nine-month span, a brand new role she delighted to play.

It was kind of a War Game called Reparations. In which, with a finely subjective eye, she cast herself as Invaded Country and Morrison as Occupying Enemy Force:

He owed her.

She collected.

He'd written a couple of industrials by then, and he figured if he did maybe three every year, he could come up with twenty to twenty-five grand, and then use the rest of his time to write shows. He had an idea; he wanted to try it.

She wanted a house. A particular house. The particular house was in Candlewood Lake, an hour and a half away from New York, an "original 1860's" brick. And of course, it had to be nicely furnished. With a maid, a pool, and a couple of cars.

And Morrison, given his own conviction that he had to keep buying a ticket to life, that if he didn't have a just-torn stub in his hand, the usher would toss him out on his ear—Morrison obliged by working his tail off, giving up all of his "free time" (the unpaid time for writing his show), and concentrated on Boy meets Car (Girl Meets Lipstick, Dog Meets Food), and finally got into scoring commercials, scoring a great Commercial Success.

His work, he once confided to Warner, was "what you could call deniably dumb." It was dumb to be writing a song to a cracker, but once you accepted that those were the rules, you could take certain pleasure in doing it well.

At least, if you weren't living with Kate.

"My husband's a serious writer," she said at a cocktail party for a Famous Author. "He Seriously writes about denture adhesive. He's very good." She turned to him. "Darling? Sing them the one about rug shampoo."

After a while he didn't care. Our Lady of Infinite Zingers, he called her. He didn't even bother to fight anymore. He was too tired.

Of almost everything. Even himself. And he felt himself slowly starting to change. From what into what, he wasn't quite sure. From living to dead. From man to machine. From lonely to even lonelier than that. But one thing he knew was, he wouldn't walk out; he wouldn't do what his father had done. He could live without tenderness, mercy, or love—but he would not *ever* walk out on his kids.

It was she who walked.

Johnathan was only two years old, and she looked around at the sprawling house (the maid, the pool, and the couple of cars) and told him he'd "trapped her" in a "gilded cage" from which, Blithe Spirit, she had to fly.

Solo, she said. He could keep the kids.

And that was the Happy Ending of that.

The last thing he'd heard, she was living in London—or was it Spain?—with Raoul, a Very Attractive Young Man whose only visible means of support was Morrison's monthly alimony checks. Checks she'd decided she had earned because: "After all, I helped you get rich, and don't ever tell me I scuttled your talent, 'cause your only talent, man of my dreams, is for making money."

IV

The telephone rang.

Morrison woke into ringing black.

It took him a second to figure it out. The ringing came from the bedside phone; the blackness came from the middle of the night. He looked at the clock. 4:17. Someone was phoning in the middle of the night. Slowly he fumbled and found the receiver.

"I hope I'm not waking you," Chalmers' voice rasped.

"Waking me," Morrison croaked out vaguely. "I think so. Hold it a second, I'll check."

He put down the phone with a loud *clunk*, and raising himself with tremendous effort, crossed to the dresser, turned on the lamp, and leaned in to squint at himself in the mirror. He rubbed his eyes. They were heavy, dazed. But certainly open. He wasn't asleep. This

47

wasn't a dream. The dog-food client had definitely called him. At exactly 4:17 A.M. Nodding slowly, he walked to the bed, sprawled on the covers, and lit up a cigarette. "No," he said to the waiting phone. "No. I'm awake. What's on your mind?"

"A brainstorm, Bobby. I had a brainstorm."

Morrison grimaced, dragging on his cigarette.

"About that spot you're recording tomorrow."

"Yeah? What about it?"

"A little change."

Morrison winced. "It better be little. The recording session's at nine-fifteen."

"I know, I know. But look, you can do it. Hey, listen, you can do anything, right? Everyday Morrison Miracles, right?"

"Meaning it's not such a little change."

"I had a vision," Chalmers intoned.

Morrison gave it some rapid thought. "God appeared in a burning bush and told you to start making Lenten dog food."

Silence. Moments of empty air. Then: "Is that supposed to be funny?"

"Uh-uh. Sorry." Morrison sighed. And for all he knew, that *had* been the vision. God grew more preposterous daily. He had to, to reach His preposterous flock.

Morrison waited, dragging on his cigarette.

"Mr. Chunky," Chalmers announced.

Morrison waited, blowing out smoke.

"Mr. *Chunky*," Chalmers repeated. "We're changing the name of the product, get it? To Mr. Chunky. And not only that, we're changing the shape. Diamonds!"

"Right. I'll cancel the session."

"No. Oh, no, You can't. You won't. I promised we'd give them a demo tomorrow. Bobby, if I don't have a demo tomorrow, I'll lose the account. I'm not joking. I've been sweating this thing for a month and a half. It's been driving me crazy. McDermott's been—"

"Stop! All right. You got it. You got it. Diamond Chunkies. You got it. You win."

"And one other thing—it's no longer a dog food."

Morrison squinted. "Do that again?"

"It's a special treat."

"What?"

"It's a special treat for your dog. The guys in marketing decided 'dog food' sounded too much like—"

"Dog food?"

"Right. So the line is: 'Not just another dog food: Mr. Chunky's a special treat.'"

Morrison nodded. "Special treat."

"Yeah. But before you do the word 'special,' do a parenthesis 'woof-woof.' A *big* woof-woof."

"A *big* woof-woof."

"Yeah, A big one. Mr. Chunky's a *hearty* dog food. I mean, it's a hearty special *treat*. So we'd like to go with some hearty woofs." Chalmers paused. "See you at nine."

"Make that eleven."

"Eleven? You can't do it sooner than that?"

"Listen. It took all *day* to build Rome." Morrison dropped the phone to its cradle and uttered a simple, hearty "Oy."

In the morning, of course, it seemed like a dream. But, shaving, he realized the obvious fact that his *life* was becoming a bad dream. Either that or a farce. Not a classy farce (Molière, Feydeau) but a television farce (*I*

Love Lucy)—a rerun, which made it infinitely worse, because the gags were stale, he'd seen them before, and he laughed at them now with a laugh-track laugh. (Nothing's funny, but these are the jokes.)

He put on his Madison Avenue outfit; gray flannel slacks, cashmere socks, Gucci shoes, and took off his new aviator glasses to slip on a cashmere turtleneck sweater. Bony, he thought, I look bony and bleary—he grimaced at himself —but gorgeously dressed.

In the kitchen, at the big butcher-block counter, the kids had already started their breakfast, and Amy looked up and said, "Morning, Daddy."

Morrison seemed to have trouble with that. *"Daddy?"* He frowned at Johnathan now. "Is this raven-haired beauty my *daughter,* sir?"

"Oh, Daddy," Johnathan said, "you're dumb."

"Well, in that case, I think I'll just shut up and eat." He frowned at their plates. "What are you eating?"

"Spaghetti."

"It can't be. It looks like spaghetti. How can you be eating spaghetti in the morning?"

"We like it," Johnathan said.

"Absurd. Completely absurd." He looked at Elsa, who stood at the stove. "My cheeseburger ready?"

"Practically, sir." She turned and frowned. "Mr. Morrison?"

"Mmm?"

She was watching him now with her soft gray eyes that identically matched her soft gray hair. "You feeling all right?"

Morrison frowned. "Of course I'm all right. Don't I look all right?"

"Extremely handsome," she said. "But tired."

"The Tragic Hero Look. Very 'in.'"

"And then"—she cleared her throat over this—"well . . . I heard you barking last night."

"Barking?" Amy was giggling now. "What were you *bark*ing for, Daddy?"

"For joy."

Johnathan giggled.

Elsa frowned. "Your father only barks for business," she said. "I figure he was working for half the night." She popped a cheeseburger onto a plate and handed it to him with a cup of coffee.

Morrison, sensing Maternal Concern, dodged her eyes and lit a cigarette. "And Johnathan helped."

"I did?"

"You did. You gave me a rhyme. 'Warm' and 'storm.'"

Johnathan grinned. The doorbell rang. Elsa said, "Eat your breakfast, I'll get it," and pushed her way through the swinging door, casting a final Motherly Glance.

Morrison, eating, turned to his daughter. "I was barking for a dog-food commercial," he said.

Balancing her elbows up on the table, she cupped her chin. "How does it go?"

He looked at her. "All right. Guess," he said. "I'll do the first part, and you can guess what the last part is."

Elsa came back with Mario Marino, a roundish man with a face that was almost deceptively sweet. He was holding a purple tie in his hand and looking disheveled, a look he'd been born with.

"'Morning," Morrison said to him now.

"We're just reviewing the dog-food commercial."

"Oh. Terrific. I can't wait to hear it." Mario smirked. "Ever since six o'clock when you called. You know what it is to change a session at—"

"Hold it. Amy and I are at work." Morrison turned to her. "Ready?"

"Set."

"Okay. It begins . . ." He started to sing, " 'Big dog flavor . . . lotsa meat . . . Mr. Chunky's a . . .' " He stopped. "A what? Three words."

Amy thought. " 'Big dog treat.' "

"Exactly." Morrison grinned at Mario. "See? So easy a child can do it. You booked the session?"

"Of course. . . . What are you eating—a *cheese*burger?"

"What does it look like?"

"A cheeseburger."

"Oh. If I'd known that, I wouldn't have eaten it. Hey—"

"How many men have you got in the session?" Amy cut in.

Mario shrugged, tying his tie. "Coupla flutes. Piano, bass, drums, and guitars. Two guitars."

"A rhythm section," Amy pronounced. "Bet you got a rhythm that's really gonna cook."

"How old is she?" Mario frowned at Morrison, who frowned at Amy. "Eight, I think. Either that or thirty. I can't remember."

"Well . . . she's awful smart for her age."

"For thirty, yeah," Morrison said. He stubbed his cigarette out and turned to his daughter. "I think you've got a dentist appointment at four. "He looked at Elsa. "Remember to take her?"

Elsa nodded. "I certainly will."

"And I'll get a good checkup," Amy announced. "It's the stannous fluoride I use in my Crest." She smiled, mischievous, baring her teeth.

Morrison grimaced. "Isn't she killingly wonderful?" he said. "She wants to grow up to star in commercials." Sighing, he stood. "Something is terribly wrong with a world where a kid wants to grow up to star in commercials." Gulping his coffee, he slammed down the cup. " 'Bye," he said. "Kids? Be good. Go to sleep."

"School," Johnathan corrected him sharply.

"School . . . sleep . . . it's the same thing."

In the cab, he was suddenly dead quiet. He sat with the guitar case propped on his lap and looked out the window at the morning traffic, which kept getting worse as they traveled down Park Avenue. At Fifty-ninth Street, seven corners of the world converged. Taxis, limousines, women on foot holding nasty umbrellas, men with briefcases, newspapers, frowns, and the office girls, young, tenderly young, rushing off to days that seemed Terribly Important, and he tilted his head, watching them now, remembering the days when days seemed Important.

"Anything bugging you?" Mario said.

Morrison turned, lifting his shoulders. "Today," he said. "I got the feeling it's gonna be bad."

"Well, so what?" Mario grinned. "It'll all be over in nine or ten hours."

"What've we got?"

Mario checked his appointment book now. "Federal Recording. Eleven o'clock. So I switched the airlines appointment to now." He looked at Morrison. "You got it?"

"The song? Does a leopard have stripes? Does a snake have feathers?"

"Wanna hum a few bars?"

"No."

"Okay."

Morrison hummed. Mario smiled. "Nice," he said, "really nice. Too good for 'em."

"Mmm."

"You got any words?"

"Yeah. Something like . . . uh . . . 'Come on to *Cal*-i-for-nia where the sun is warm . . . come with me, we'll fly there, baby—' "

" *'Baby'*?" Mario said. *"Baby*?" I think you've been reading your own publicity."

"Oh." Morrison flushed. "You're right. It's just that I wanted the flying line there. I mean, *they're* gonna want the flying line there. If I didn't have to put the flying line there, I could. . . . Forget it. I'll think of something else."

"You got seven minutes." Mario sighed and looked through the window. "How do you like that rotten creep?"

Morrison turned. *"Which* rotten creep?"

"Chalmers. Calling you at four in the morning. Why didn't you just hang up on the jerk?"

"Hell, I don't know." Morrison laughed. "He started flaunting his mortgage at me. And his kid's orthodontia. And do I want to be responsible for bringing another buck-toothed teenager into the world. That kind of thing."

"Old Softie," Mario said.

"Right," Morrison agreed. "I'm stupid."

The cab pulled up at the given address—a classy, glassy hulk of a tower, home of Rush & McFadden Inc. Mario paid and got out of the cab. Morrison followed, lugging his guitar and wondering what, and who, he'd be meeting. There were advertising men, and Advertising Men. There were guys who were smart and human and funny—usually the writers and the art directors—and then there were the guys who were dull and dumb—the executives, account men, the marketing experts, the guys who didn't see a woman as a woman, but as part of, for instance, The Peanut Butter Market. Hamilton Rush was one of those guys.

Morrison stopped, to chain-light a cigarette, and then, nodding at Mario, walked through the door. They walked through the cool, marbled lobby, with fluorescent lighting and plastic plants, and planted themselves at the elevator bank that was labeled *30 to 44.*

Mario was humming "California." "Catchy," he said. "Really nice."

The meeting was impossible.

"I don't believe it," Morrison said. They were sitting in a coffee-shop booth with Warner. "I don't believe what happened up there."

Warner just nodded, scratching his beard. "How long have you been in this business?" he asked.

"Seven years."

"Seven years. And you don't believe it?"

"You're right. I believe it," Morrison said. He looked at Mario. "Tell him what happened."

"Fools in where others fear to tread," Morrison snapped. And then: "Go on. Go on, Mario. Sorry. Go on."

"Rush—"

"Rush heard the tune," Mario said. "It's gorgeous. It's really gorgeous. It flies. Bob paints a picture of sunsets, and mountains, and palm trees and surf that could make you weep. And the last line comes . . . something-something, 'wherever you roam . . .'" Mario sang, "Cal-i-*for*-nia keeps *call*-ing you *home*. . . .'" He looked at Warner. "Beautiful, right? I mean, I wanna go back there and I never even *been* there. You know what I mean?"

"Yeah. And so *Rush* says . . ." Warner prompted.

"Yeah. And so *Rush* says, 'It really soars. It really takes off.' And then he looks at Bob and says, 'Problem is that it doesn't land.'"

"Land?" Warner said.

"As in 'ever come down,'" Morrison explained. "The exact words were, 'When our planes take off to music like that, I get the vision they'll never come back. That heaven's doors will open and swallow them. . . .'"

Warner just stared.

"I can tell you think that's the punch line, too." Morrison grinned.

"No?"

"No. You want some more coffee?"

"No. It's awful."

"Right." Morrison ordered more coffee. The waitress gave him a greasy smile and pulled a pencil from behind an ear that was slightly scented with Jungle perfume. She added the check up and walked away.

"The punch line was," Morrison said, "the

agency's handling another product that they thought the tune would be perfect for."

"A product that soars?"

"A product whose image they wanted to raise."

Warner cocked his head. "Do I want to hear this?"

"No. I don't think so," Morrison said.

"Good. Then let's go." Warner stood up. "We've got a recording at—"

"Toilet-bowl cleaner," Morrison said. He lifted his glasses and rubbed his eyes. "A freshening process."

"Freshening process?" Warner squinted. What is a freshening process?"

"Toilet-bowl cleaner," Morrison said.

"Oh."

"Mmm. It's a new phrase. Seven people took seven months to come up with that phrase. But they wrote the jingle right on the spot. Just like that. And they practically fit it into the tune." Morrison took a sip of his coffee. "Wanna hear it?" he said.

"No."

"Good. It goes . . . 'Be-*hind* your bathroom do-or. O-dors just won't *live* there *an-y-more.* . . .' "

Warner stared at him. "You're kidding," he breathed.

"I wish that I were."

Warner laughed.

Morrison started to get up from the table, and something hot, sharp, and nasty raced through his chest and stabbed him in the heart. It pushed him back to the vinyl seat.

Mario was frowning. "Hey. What's the matter?"

Morrison winced. The pain lightened, eased, flew away. "Nothing," he said. "Acid indigestion. 'Coffee kickback.' Something like that."

"Lousy coffee," Mario said. "C'mon. We got a date with a couple of dogs."

V

They walked to Federal. The blinking lights
on the IBM Building said it was eighteen degrees and ten-forty-five. The wind bit. Morrison could hear himself breathing. So I must be
alive; he tried to laugh. But the pain had
had scared him. He never went to doctors. Because as a kid he'd been to too many. The
rheumatic fever had kept him at home, in bed
for six months, and out of school for the rest
of the year. And then, after that, his mother
kept insisting he be "checked up" every seven
minutes, or at least so it seemed. There were
no lesions on his heart. But there were things
about which he was supposed to "be careful."

Like smoking. And working himself around
the clock.

They were waiting for the light on the corner of Fifth when Morrison spotted a pretzel

vendor, an old man, with mouton earmuffs and a seaman's jacket, standing in front of a rolling cart. He told the others to go on ahead, he had to buy pretzels. Mario nervously eyed his watch. "He's being an eccentric artiste," Warner said, but he looked up sharply. "You *are* gonna show?"

Morrison nodded. "Have I ever not shown?"

"Most reliable man in the business," Warner said, and grabbing Mario, they made the light.

Morrison bought a bag of pretzels, and seriously thought about not showing up. Just taking the pretzel bag to the airport, checking it through, and flying to Madrid; or Buenos Aires.

Where the sun was warm.

But he'd always shown up. Most reliable man in the business.

Right.

"Hey, Morrison? Bob Morrison. Right?"

The man in front of him was short and dark and losing his hair. "Hey. Don't you remember me?" he said.

Morrison squinted. The face was familiar, but only slightly. An account executive, he thought. On what? A diet cola with better taste? A compact car with better mileage?

"Brookman," the man said. "Leonard Brookman."

Morrison squinted.

"D House? School? You used to play our fraternity parties."

"Oh, yeah," Morrison said. "Oh, yeah." And then, because he couldn't think of anything else, he said, "Great to see you. What're you doing?"

"Me? I sell recording equipment."

If Ever I See You Again

"Well, that's great. I sell pretzels," Morrison said. He extended the bag. "Want one?"

Brookman chuckled. "I know what you're doing. I read all about you in *TV Guide*."

"Oh."

"He said modestly." Brookman laughed. "So tell me. You ever see any of the guys?"

Morrison grinned. Brookman's "guys" would be guys like Kenny Larkin, or Ralph Schotz, or What's-his-face, whose father owned Nicaragua, or sold bananas there, or something like that.

"Hardly anyone," Morrison said.

It was getting late. But given a choice between talking the Bad Old Days with Brookman or facing Chalmers, Morrison stayed.

"I still see Schiffrin," Brookman announced, shaking his head. "Good old Schiffrin. And Jerry Brown. Remember him?"

"The D House Clown."

"That's what we called him. Yeah, that's the guy. He's a neighbor of mine in Larchmont."

"Oh." Morrison nodded. Amazing what a man would do, he thought, to avoid a simple recording session.

Brookman said, "What about Davey Miller? I remember you used to be friends with him, right? You ever see him?"

"Yeah. All the time." Morrison shrugged. "You can see him, too. He's playing at Carnegie Hall this week."

"Yeah? No kidding?"

"Saturday night."

"Playing *piano?*"

"That, or poker. They often play poker at Carnegie Hall."

Brookman grinned. "Yeah. I remember you

always had a mouth." The wind was lifting some strands of his hair, and he patted them down. "Yeah. And Davey always loved the piano. Whaddya know. Carnegie Hall." He grinned even wider. "But I bet you make enough to *buy* Carnegie Hall. Right?"

Dog food was suddenly better. "I have to go now," Morrison said.

Brookman nodded. "Yeah. Me too. Too bad you didn't get to last month's reunion."

"Yeah. Well, I really have to—"

"Thirteen years." Brookman shook his head. "I ask you, who else but our nutty class would have something nutty like a thirteenth reunion." He shook his head again. "Everyone was there."

A blond went by with a Bendel's shopping bag slung on her arm. For no particular reason, she smiled. The kind of smile that could make a man's day.

"Bloomgarten, Kirkwood, Hammersmith, Slade . . . and the *girls*—man, you shoulda seen Rosalind Wilkers. Fat? And then the gorgeous one, What's-her-name . . . Jennifer . . ."

Morrison blinked. *"Corley?"* And found it completely amazing that the sound of her name could still make him feel . . . dumb.

"Nah. She was only a sophomore. No. Jennifer Robbins is the one I mean. Robbins, yeah. That was her name. But funny you should mention Jennifer Corley. Ran into her, oh, say, three months ago. She was here on a visit."

"Oh," he said. And then found himself adding with a *chuckle*, "Here with her husband and seventeen kids?"

"I don't know." Brookman shrugged. "Alone when I met her. She lives in California. Malibu, I think. Hey, listen, man, we gotta get together sometime."

"Yeah." Brookman was handing him a card. Morrison took it. "Yeah," he repeated.

"Well . . . great to see you," Brookman was saying.

"Yeah. Great." Morrison said. And put the card carefully away in his pocket, as though there were some kind of Message in it.

The light changed.

He crossed the street.

Federal Recording had changed overnight. The reception room was a reception room now, and instead of the blond hatcheck girl, a receptionist, a middle-aged lady named Ruth, sat behind the vinyl desk drinking coffee. She looked pretty pooped, but she waved at Morrison. "Welcome to the land of the half-living."

He took off his coat now, lighting a cigarette. "Too much party last night?" he asked.

"At my age, *any* party's too much."

"But especially that one," Morrison said.

"Especially that one." Ruth shook her head. "Mario said to tell you he left, and you're in Studio C," she said, "if you care."

"C for Chalmers. . . . He here yet?"

"Mmm. Got somebody with him named—" She looked at her book—"Merriweather and Ford."

"That's two somebodies."

"Wanna bet?"

Morrison poured some bad-looking coffee from a giant Silex that sat on a shelf. "You wouldn't have any real milk?"

"Nope. Just the nice, powdery white stuff. . . . It's low-cholesterol," she added.

"No sale."

In Control Room C, Jim, the engineer, was racking the tape. He was young, and wearing a red flannel shirt, and drinking a Coke. He knew his business, and the look on his face told Morrison all was not going well. Nothing could be read on Warner's face. Which was why Warner was good at his job. Warner was leaning on the edge of the console, nodding at Chalmers and two other men. Chalmers was his usual doughy-faced self. The other two guys looked like an ex-marine and a third V.P. of a Kansas bank. Though not necessarily in that order.

Warner looked up as Morrison entered and, smilingly, introductions were made. The Kansas banker was Merriweather—the client. Mr. Dog Food himself. The other one, Ford, was the assistant client. And in answer to Morrison's question, they were "fine."

The musicians were starting to assemble in the studio. Fat Irving set up his drums. Morrison started to excuse himself.

"Bob?" Merriweather: smiling.

Morrison smiled, looking impatient.

"Mr. Merriweather's got a little thing he wants to tell you." Warner smiled. "A little marketing thing."

Morrison smiled. "Well, I think Mr. Chalmers has told me all that, and the song's been written—"

"Well, actually," Chalmers interjected smoothly, "it's more of an *emotional* thing he wants to tell you."

Morrison looked at the dog-food client, who looked as though he would not get emotional

if he saw a tractor running over a kid. Or
even a dog.

"The emotional climate," he now said to
Morrison, "is very important in selling this
product. What we want to emphasize is large
chunks of meat. Very little cereal and large
chunks of meat."

"Right," said Ford.

"Right," said Morrison. He looked through
the wide glass window of the booth. The musicians were already scanning the charts. He
started moving to the studio now.

"Just a *second*," Merriweather said sharply,
and Morrison turned. Merriweather coughed.
"The point is—and I think this is very important—we'd like the music to sound chunky."

"Chunky." Morrison was rooted to the spot.
"Chunky," he repeated.

"Yes, chunky," Merriweather said. "Not
thin and watery. I was thinking . . . if you
added one of those—oh, you know what I mean
—one of those oversized violins."

Slowly Morrison turned to Warner. "I don't
know what he means. Do you know what he
means?"

"I think he means a bass," Warner said
slowly.

"Exactly," Merriweather said, "a bass. They
could plunk on them a little, and I think it
would sound very meaty that way."

"Yeah . . . well. I don't have that kind of
bass. I have *that* kind of bass." Morrison
pointed through the glass window at Wilkerson, holding the fender bass.

"Well, then, let's order some," Chalmers
said.

"And some of those big violins," Ford added.

"Big violins?" Morrison asked.

"For a big sound. And how about bassoons? And maybe a tuba," Merriweather said. "Now *that* is *really* a big sound."

Morrison put his coffeecup down, lifted his glasses, and rubbed his eyes. "Look, I don't . . . I don't have those instruments, and even if I did, I don't know what they'd play. I mean, the parts have to be *written* for the instruments, see. I mean, the guys don't just fall in here and . . . Look, what I mean is, why don't we just go with what we've got. We got the guys here, and the studio, and the music, and let's go."

"With what?" Chalmers asked. "What have you got?"

Morrison pointed. "Guitars, bass, piano, flutes—"

"Flutes?" Chalmers said.

"Big flutes," Morrison assured him. "About *that* big," he said, spreading his hands. "And to sing the song, I've got two people. Two very big people. So now I'm gonna work." He turned and left, hearing Merriweather say, "I feel we've got a lack of communication."

He entered the studio, shaking his head. He could not say anything, or even scream, because at any moment, at the flick of a button, he might be overheard from the control-room speaker. He looked at Charas, who was at the piano. Charas was a damn good jazz pianist, who, like everyone else, got hungry and played commercials. It was easy enough if you just did the playing. You came in for an hour, kept your face on straight when the craziness

66

started (and even if you didn't, who cared —after all, you were only a crazy musician), and then you collected residual checks.

Charas was keeping his face on straight.

But he was crossing his eyes.

Morrison laughed. He turned to Spender, on lead guitar. Spender was black and completely bald. Spender said, "Nu?"

"I'll give you guys *four*," Morrison said. "Okay? Then we'll—"

"Bob?" Voice through the speaker: Warner. Morrison turned.

"Bob?" Warner stood, leaning over the console. Smiling. "Bob, could you come here a second?"

"Look, I'd just like to run this through. Once. Okay? Then I'll be—"

"Bob, could you come here *now*?"

"Right."

In the control room, Morrison picked up his cold coffee and lit a cigarette. "What?" he said.

"Tubas," Warner said. "Mr. Merriweather feels very, very, very strongly about tubas. And basses. That you can plunk on. So I think . . . we ought to order some."

"Order some," Morrison said. "Swell. Terrific. And while we're at it, I'd like to order a few composers. Big composers."

"What?" Chalmers said.

"Composers. They're like recorders, only bigger. Woodwinds," he explained, and then, turning to Jim, the kid-engineer: "All right. Would you do me a trip downstairs? Ask the girl to round up a couple of basses, no tubas, and hold the mayo."

"That's a good idea," Merriweather said.

"While we're waiting, we could order some lunch." He looked at Morrison. "Would you order me a Coke and pastrami on white?"

Morrison stood there squinting at the man. The man was asking him to order a lunch. It was no big thing. It was not a big deal. Lerner, maybe, ordered lunch for Loewe. Gershwin, maybe, ordered lunch for Kaufman. Rimski, maybe, ordered lunch for Korsakov. A man had to be a pretty small man with a pretty big ego to not order lunch.

"I don't do that," Morrison said, keeping his voice as flat as he could. "I'm not in the waiters' union," he said. And the quick hot pain ran straight through his chest.

"Bob?" The engineer tapped him on the arm. "I'll take care of it. You want something too?"

"I lost my appetite," Morrison breathed, gripping the console. The pain went away. He jerked his head at Warner, as the ad men started to place their orders. "Listen," he whispered, "I think I'm gonna walk."

"You mean *go* for a walk," Warner said warily.

"I think I mean walk," Morrison said. "Quit. Leave. End. 'Bye."

"C'mon." Warner frowned. "I'll walk you to the hall.

"What you need is a rest," Warner said in the hall. "Just take some time off."

"A vacation won't help me."

"Vacation? Hell. I don't *mean* a vacation. Take the afternoon off." Warner grinned. "I'll get Stakowsky to conduct the session."

"Expand his horizons."

"Something like that. And listen, while you're out, will you get me a sandwich? I think

I'm up for baloney on wry—and that's spelled with a 'w.' "

Morrison wasn't in the mood to laugh. A state of mind he found suddenly refreshing.

Warner said, "C'mon. Stop looking so grim. It's only the usual everyday crud."

"But why is every day usually crud?"

"Oh . . ." Warner sighed, rolling his eyes. "You really want me to answer that question? Philosophers have pondered that one for years."

"Yeah. So have I. But I'm probably stupid. I don't even have a philosophy."

"Sure. Sure you're stupid." Warner cocked his head. "If you're so stupid, how come you ain't poor?"

"Cute." Morrison grimaced slightly. He put on his coat.

Warner frowned. "Happiness can't buy money," he said.

"Cute. I'll see you."

"When?"

"Later."

"I'll meet you at Captivation at four."

"Maybe," Morrison said at the door.

"Be there."

"Maybe," Morrison said.

VI

Eleven-thirty, Luncheon-hour traffic hadn't begun. The streets still belonged to the idle rich. And the idle poor. In the window of Bonwit's, across Fifth Avenue, the models wore "Home for the Holiday" clothes—long, silky, clingy little dresses, and satin pajamas, and bows in their hair, and the women on the streets looked hurried and cross, and in front of the entrance, a toothless black man held up a cup and a hand-lettered sign: THANK GOD YOU CAN SEE. Morrison slipped him a ten-dollar bill, saying, "It's a ten," and then suddenly winced, thinking he sounded like a lousy show-off. Some days you just couldn't win with yourself.

He walked up Fifth now, feeling embarrassed—embarrassed for staging that idiot talk. And he suddenly remembered Leonard

If Ever I See You Again

Brookman, a scene back at D House. "That's
what we pay you for—music. Right?" Brookman had said. And nothing had changed.
That's what he sold. Music as Commodity. The
going rate; fifty bucks a note. (Half-price for
half-notes.)

And why the hell not?

He passed the Plaza, its fountain, deserted.
The sky was gray, threatening rain. A bag
lady sat on a bench in the park.

And there was nothing more poignant, more
moving, more—Yea—even universally touch-
ing than a man with sixty-five grand in his
bank account wailing to heaven and mourn-
ing his fate. Farce, he thought, and waved for
a taxi.

You could hear the music from the downstairs hall. It was mixed with the odor of boil-
ing cabbage, and the sound of a grease-
throated television voice, giving *"a brand-new
Lincoln Continental, and a full year's supply of
Dishwasher All."* A woman appeared from a
first-floor apartment carrying garbage and a
small yellow dog. Morrison pictured the dog in
the trashcan, the woman intently walking her
garbage.

Which proved he at least wasn't losing his
mind.

Yet.

He climbed up the wooden stairs. Climbed
and climbed. The piano music was getting
louder, more distinct, more . . . God, it was
gorgeous. He stopped for a moment on the
fourth-floor landing, catching the lousy racket
of his heart. It sounded like he'd just been rac-

ing a marathon. Four lousy flights. He'd been smoking too much. He rang the doorbell of Davey's apartment.

The music continued. Sonata Thirty-One; Opus One-Eleven: Beethoven.

Laura answered the door, smiled, kissing him.

He moaned. "Don't tell me that's Jungle perfume?"

She grinned. "Can't resist you, kid. Never could."

"Right. You just married Davey on the rebound." Morrison dumped his coat in the hallway. The music soared through the living-room arch. "So what's he doing?" Morrison said.

"Now?"

"Uh-huh."

"I don't know. Haven't seen him. The maid's in the living room dusting the piano. I'll look in the kitchen. Would you like some coffee?"

"Nice." He entered the living room now. A clean, light, airy room with well-worn furniture and well-fed plants. Davey looked up but continued to play. Morrison sat on a brown tweed sofa and watched him. Davey hadn't changed very much. He was still skinny, his face was still boyish, and his thin dark hair fell over his eyes.

"Very effective," Morrison said.

"Glad you like it."

"The hair in your eyes, I mean. Very arty."

Davey mouthed something pleasantly obscene. He stopped playing. "So. How'd you manage a free afternoon?"

"Don't ask."

"All right." Davey nodded pleasantly.

"I thought I could put some lyrics to your song."

"Song?"

"That catchy tune you were playing. How about . . . ? Got it!" Morrison sang to the Beethoven music, " 'Mr. Chunky can't be beat. Lotsa flavor, lotsa meat.' "

Davey nodded. "One of those days, huh?"

Laura came back and handed out coffee. "You look tired," she said.

"A dog phoned me at four in the morning." Morrison sipped. "That's terrific," he said. "Real coffee flavor."

Laura frowned. "They really called you at four A.M.?"

"Oh, wow." Davey pounded a dissonant chord. "Will you look at the sympathy? Listen, he picked it." He looked at Morrison. "You asked for it, right?"

Morrison nodded. "With my own little hatchet." He rubbed his eyes. "You rehearsed at the hall yet?"

Davey lit up. "Yesterday. Just went to check the acoustics." He sighed. "You ever been in that hall?"

"I am not a cultural cretin. Yes. If you're asking if I've ever *played* there, no."

"I'm telling you"—Davey was shaking his head—"it's an absolute wonder, that place. The sound—oh, Bobby, the sound, the sound. It goes all the way up to the end of the theater . . . and then it bounces right back at you. I mean, it's a dream. I mean it's like . . . picture a beautiful woman . . . a really, really beautiful woman . . . a woman you know you're never gonna have. And then one day, whammo— there she is, and not only that, she's saying,

'I love you,' and the sound goes way up to the rafters and bounces back at you. That's what it's like."

"Who's the woman?" Laura said flatly.

"Don't worry," Davey said. "She can't cook."

"Wonderful," Laura said. "Terrific. You give a man the sexiest years of your life, and all he remembers is your oatmeal cookies."

Davey said, "You got any oatmeal cookies?"

And Laura said no, but she'd hustle up lunch, to which Morrison, of course, was welcome to stay.

It was a fine lunch. A cheese omelet and a tossed green salad and hot buttered rolls and a bottle of wine. And when Laura cleared the table, Morrison announced that he'd better eat and run and let David rehearse, but Davey shook his head. "Why don't the gentlemen withdraw to the withdrawing room for brandy and cigars?" He picked up his coffee and walked to the living room.

Morrison followed. "You got some kind of problem you want to discuss?"

"Yeah. Yours."

"Mine."

"The one you came here to discuss."

"Oh," Morrison said, "that one. Actually, I think I came here to forget it." He shrugged. "And besides, it's just something dumb. Like what am I doing with my life."

"Oh. That one." Davey nodded, sitting on the couch. "Well . . . you're free to do anything you like."

"Yeah." Morrison sat down beside him. "Exactly. So tell me—why don't I do it?"

"Maybe you just don't know what it is?"

74

Morrison thought about that for a while. "How about nothing? Could I do nothing?"

Davey thought. "I doubt it," he said. "How about going back to the theater?"

Morrison whooped. "Without a ticket, they won't let me in. Listen, as far as Broadway is concerned, I'm a rank amateur, accent on the 'rank.'"

"Bull." Davey stood up to pace. "You wrote two shows."

"*Sure* I did. Now hear it, baby. *Blitz* was the worst thing to happen in a theater since Booth shot Lincoln, and *Kleinman in Love,* if you remember that one, the year before *Blitz*—"

"I remember the reviews said the score was brilliant."

"But the patient died." Morrison laughed. "It closed in Philly after seventeen minutes."

"Which wasn't your fault."

"That, and a nickel, don't even buy coffee." Morrison paused, leaning back on the couch, watching as Davey strode through the room. "And besides," he said slowly, "I wouldn't even want to do that again. You write something good—or maybe it's not good—but you never get to know because twenty-seven people keep changing it around. All worlds are just like advertising, kid." He blew out a smoke ring. "Except for yours."

Davey nodded, looking at his hands. "Nobody rewrites Beethoven. True." He looked up slowly. "But few people hum him in the shower, either. All I'm saying is, you know how to turn out tunes people hum. And you know how to move them. Not just to drugstores or car lots or Caribbean islands, I mean, just *move* them. So do it, baby. And do it for film. Really, it strikes me as the obvious thing. I mean, that's what you've been doing for the last seven years, and that's what you really *do* like a genius. So do it. Get your rear out to California."

Morrison sat there smiling benignly.

"What's so amusing?" Davey said. "It's what's you ought to do."

"And just for the record, I tried to do it." Davey sat down again, frowning attention, as Morrison continued, "About a year ago. I . . . uh . . . applied for the job, as it were. I mean, I let them know that Marvelous Melodious Morrison Music was now available for motion pictures. Suitable for framing on the giant screen."

"And?"

"The earthquake they had that year was caused by everybody yawning at once."

"Come on." Davey frowned.

"Come on, yourself. The general response to my list of credits was, 'Yeah, but we don't *make* films about toothpaste.' "

"Oh, man. You've done—"

"Forget it!" Morrison's voice sounded sharp. He flattened it. "Just forget it, huh?"

Davey nodded solemnly once, then knuckled his jaw. "So what'll you do?"

"Well . . ." Standing, Morrison stretched, till he felt the muscles pop in his back. He yawned. "Play hookey for the rest of the day, and then work, I guess. I'm scoring a film for Buick tomorrow. A fugue for crankshaft, spark plugs, and horns. Wanna come?"

"No, thanks. I cry at funerals."

"Yeah," Morrison said. "So did I."

VII

The neon sign blinked CAPTIVATION in red,
white, blue, and then red again. The cabdriver
squinted out through the window, and then
turned around to Morrison.

"Fifteen-twenty-seven Broadway," he said.
"This what you want? A penny arcade?"

"That's what I want," Morrison said. He
leaned forward in the lumpy seat, trying to
peer through the heavy bulletproof-plastic
partition to see what the meter had to say.
3.95.

Patently absurd. He pulled out a five, and
the driver started the old eye war. The game
of avoiding Morrison's eye for so long he'd
leave without asking for change. Morrison
said, "Give me twenty-five cents," which the
driver gave him, along with a glare. Flipping
the quarter, he stepped from the cab.

Broadway glittered like an overdressed hooker. She was sad and painted and down on her luck, an underdog too unregenerate to root for, but you had to, if only because she was honest. Broadway was rotten, but at least she didn't lie.

The penny arcade smelled of caramel popcorn, with just the faintest overlay of grass. The customers were mostly winos and kids. It was twenty to four, and Warner wasn't there.

Morrison stuck his quarter in a Blippo, a pinball game that blipped when you won. Morrison lost, and went to the change booth. Behind him, somebody laughed very hard. He went back to Blippo and fed it with silver, moving the flippers with dexterous hands. The machine went crazy, spitting out coins. It made him angry. He'd wanted to lose.

He walked away from it, leaving the money, and a couple of pock-faced Puerto Rican kids made a dash for it. Morrison bought some popcorn.

And started to think about Jennifer Corley.

He had not been thinking about Jennifer Corley so hard all day that not thinking about her had become an obsession. And now she popped up, in the middle of his mind, in the middle of a Broadway penny arcade, blinking out red-white-and-blue CAPTIVATION.

Kid stuff.

A one-night stand.

A comedy.

Intense Young Man meets Homecoming Queen.

But he couldn't dismiss it as easily as that. Maybe, he thought, the First Time always leaves a scar on your heart. Or a hole in your head. Or a kick in your gut. Not the first time of sex; that wasn't it. The first time of sex was a simple, physical rite of passage. Today I am a man. But the first time of love—he remembered it clearly—was a passage into something very close to awe. For a very quiet second, the world seemed splendid, and the splendid message was: Today I'm Not Alone.

And that was a feeling he'd never had since. Jennifer Corley.

"So. You having a nice nap?" Warner stood there, head to the side, his Gucci briefcase up on a Blippo. "For a second you looked like you might be dreaming. Of firebombing Madison Avenue, I trust?"

Ignoring him, Morrison said, "Pick your game."

Warner looked around, seeming to find it a difficult choice. There were Shoot-the-Ducks and Toss-the-Rings and a lineup of weird mechanical games. The air whanged, pinged, blipped.

"I'll make it air hockey," Warner said.

"Right. And we'll make it a nickel a game." They walked to the long, flat table and rented a couple of palm-size paddles and a plastic puck. Warner had a strange expression on his face: something between a smirk and a grin. "I don't think you're gonna *believe* what happened after you left."

"I will, but I don't want to hear it. Play ball."

The puck went whizzing across the table, and Morrison shot it back.

"You sure?"

"Don't wanna hear nothin' to do with business, okay? This is my day off."

"Okay." Warner was still looking funny. "Okay. So what did *you* do today?"

"Went to Davey's." Morrison made a lousy return. "Forgot to tell you—I ran into Brookman."

"Who?"

"Lovable Leonard Brookman. School. D House."

Warner fumbled, missing a shot.

"He was standing on the corner of Fifty-seventh. He's selling tape decks and lives in Larchmont."

"Sounds like fun."

"Mmm."

"How did you know who he was?"

"I didn't. He came gunning for me. He saw my picture in *TV Guide*."

"He was properly impressed."

Morrison nodded. "He was always stupid."

"Come off it."

"What?"

"Being so I-don't-care. It's a nice piece. You come off terrific. 'Modest,' 'romantic,' 'sardonic . . .'"

"Yeah, that's me." Morrison laughed. "So I'm being modest and sardonic about it."

"Why don't you just, as they say, relax and enjoy it?"

Morrison looked up. "Because I'm being pretentiously self-involved and comically tragic this week—how's that for an objective eye?— and tomorrow I'll return to my old jolly self. And tomorrow I'll say, 'Whoopee. That'll show Miss Peters from the seventh grade, and Rosalie Birnbaum, whose mother didn't want her to date me in high school because I—quote—'had no future,' unquote, but today I'm regressing to Youthful Intensity and I'll thank you to keep your good cheer to yourself."

Warner thought, putting down his paddle. "You weren't particularly intense as a youth."

"Like hell I wasn't. Man. I went around playing Heathcliff—morose meanderings out on the moors. Dark moods and matching turtleneck sweaters." Morrison lobbed a terrific shot.

Warner returned it. "Well, you were doing that senior year. But I attributed that to the Lady Corley."

"Sure. Right. She broke my heart. Had it on my sleeve, and she bumped it with a cafeteria tray."

Warner studied him, suddenly grinned. "Listen. I bet as we stand here now, she's reading the article, eating her heart out, thinking: my God, if I hadn't dropped him for—what was that moron's name?"

"Kenny Larkin."

"He happens to remember. Thinking: If I hadn't dropped him for Kenny, I'd be sharing all this excitement now."

"This is excitement?"

"To *her* it is"—Warner lobbed out a shot —"in her small, depressing suburban tract house—"

"Filled with roaches and squalling brats—"

"Her dentures about to be repossessed—"

"Her husband, who works in a garlic factory—"

"Right," Warner said. "To her, I think it

might be exciting to be married to a man who's flying to Hollywood Friday morning on flight one-eleven at nine-fifteen to go to a meeting with Soznick and Foster at three-twenty-five P.M. at Soznick's mansion in Beverly Hills to talk about scoring their latest feature entitled *If Ever I See You Again,* a major nine-million-dollar feature which happens to require a couple of songs—to a schlepper like her, it might be exciting."

Morrison stood there rubbing his jaw. "Do that again?"

"Right," Warner said. "To her, I think it might be excit—"

"Just the last part."

"No. You don't want to talk business today."

Mario said, "So that was it. They saw the thingy in *TV Guide* and you're suddenly the hottest item in the world. The man who knows how to move the millions."

"The man who makes strong women weep," Warner added.

Morrison turned in his baseball chair and looked at Amy, who was dancing around him.

"Daddy's gonna score a movie," she sang.

"Not necessarily," Mario said. He lifted his shoulders. "Very probably," he added quickly, "but you never can tell with those Hollywood guys."

Amy said, "What's wrong with Hollywood guys?"

"The same thing that's wrong with everyone else. Only, the sun makes it grow a lot bigger." Warner smiled. "Anyway, they're buying a round-trip ticket and they want to see you."

"To give me a script?"

"Man, I don't know what they'll give you. Maybe they'll give you a hard time. Any rate, why don't you stay for the weekend, do some relaxing, get in some sun."

"Davey's concert is Saturday night. I've got to make a plane back Saturday morning."

"Yeah . . . that's really rotten timing."

"It's wonderful timing. What do you mean?"

"That you could use a vacation," Mario squinted. "You been to a doctor lately?"

"What's the matter? I look like I'm dying or something?"

"How about a checkup?"

"How about a shutup?" Morrison looked at his watch and then up at Amy. "How about bed?"

"Rhymes with 'wed.' Also with 'dead.' "

"Right. And also with you better go 'ahead,' because Daddy 'said.' "

"Will you come in later?"

"Have I ever missed a night?"

"Yes," she said. "When you were dating Molly."

"Get out of here," he laughed. "Get out, get out."

When she left, Mario, yawning, stood up. "So I'll book us a flight back on Saturday morning and I'll see you tomorrow at the Buick—"

"Hold it. What is this 'us'?" Morrison was lighting a new cigarette, and paused, with his lighter burning the air. "You trying to tell me you'll be on the plane?"

"Listen, Bob. If they start talking money, I don't want them to talk directly to you. You gotta play high above the money scene, right?"

"Hey, look. I want to do a picture so badly, I'd do it for nothing."

"That's what I'm afraid of. . . . See you to-morrow."

Warner stood up. "Go to sleep," he said. "And pleasant dreams about California. Land of honey, lotus, and palm."

And Jennifer Corley, Morrison thought.

And wished he could kick himself in the teeth.

Refrain

VIII

"Jen?"

"Mmm?" She rolled over to her back. The deck chair was burning hot from the sun. She was getting lotion all over the canvas.

"You coming to the Cortlands' or not?"

She opened her eyes. Tom was standing on the porch getting dressed, tucking his shirt down into his slacks. Beautiful shirt, beautiful slacks, beautiful Tom.

"Do you want me to—no, let me put it this way—do you *need* me to come?"

"Well"—he shrugged—"it's ten million bucks' worth of business, Jen. If Cortland decides to build that hotel—"

"It certainly won't be because of me."

"No. But he likes to see pretty ladies . . ."

"Mmm," she said, and wondered what would

happen if she went to the party, pretty, and suddenly stood on her head in the middle of the Cortlands' dining-room table, or emptied the ashtrays into the soup. Would it help that she was pretty?

"Listen," he said. "Yes or no. I don't have all day."

"All right," she said. "What time is it?"

"Twenty minutes to three."

"I meant, what time is the Cortland thing?"

"Oh. Six. It's casual," he added.

"Aren't we all." She suddenly laughed.

"What's that supposed to mean?"

"Nothing," she laughed. "That's why it's casual. Because it means nothing."

He nodded slowly, running a comb through his thick black hair. "Another cryptic evening with Jennifer Corley."

"I'm not trying to be cryptic," Jennifer said. "I'm just being myself."

"Yeah. Well, that's cryptic enough for me."

"I know," she said. And her voice held neither sadness nor pleasure. She reached for a Coke from the redwood table at the side of her chaise. He was fumbling car keys out of his pocket.

"So, will you pick me up, or shall I pick you up, or what?" he said.

She sipped some Coke, and then, closing her eyes, rested the can on her bare midriff. It was cold and wet against the heat of her skin. "I'll pick you up at your house," she said. "At seven."

"I don't want to be late."

"If we get there at *ten*, we'll still be early.

You know they won't serve a thing till eleven. Except too many drinks."

"All right," he said. "All right. Six-thirty." And lying there, with her eyes still closed, she heard him starting to walk down the steps.

She could let him go. With her eyes wide *open*, she could let him go, as he could let her go, and knowing that clearly, she could let him stay. And yet, she was always uncomfortably aware of a deeper, darker, less flattering truth: she needed him—because she did not need him.

Rising from the chaise, she went after him now, catching him standing on the edge of the driveway.

"Hey, I'm sorry," she said to him. "Hey, I've really got some kind of bug on, I guess. It's just that—"

"I know. You've been working too hard." His brown eyes studied her, frowning slightly.

She nodded. "But Park's is an important gallery. And I just want everything right for the show. I had to do frames for all of those pictures, and then when I'd gotten the grubwork done, I rewarded myself by starting a painting."

"And you worked all night."

"Something like that."

He sighed at her, still shaking his head. "Is it good?"

"I think so."

"Can I see it?"

"When it's done."

He shrugged. "I won't understand it, anyway."

"I know. Poor darling. And you hunt so

89

hard for the adjectives, too." She smiled at him nicely. " 'Firm' . . . 'kinetic' . . . 'interesting' . . ."

"Well, I *do* think your work is interesting."

"And I . . ." She was going to say "think yours is interesting too," but it was too early in the day to start lying. Or too late. "I'll see you at six," she said, and kissed him; and kissed him again through the window of the car.

Climbing back up the steep wooden steps, she sipped some more Coke, and then leaned on the railing, looking at the strip of sand down below. The Pacific Ocean was her front lawn and, smiling, she thought: it never needs watering. The sun felt wonderful, hot but gentle; it painted the cottage with jagged pieces of shadow and gold.

My castle, she thought, my Place in the Sun.

It was a fine cottage of unpainted pine. Twenty-eight steps led up to the porch that looked at the ocean. The neighboring houses were far enough away to give it a pleasant illusion of aloneness.

Stretching, she grabbed her towel from the chaise and, noticing Tom had left his watch on the table, she picked it up, yawning, and banged through the door.

Inside the living room was orderly, spare. A shelf full of books and records on the left, an upright piano that had come with the house, sailcloth sofa, glass table, small hooked rug on the varnished floor, undraped windows that she thought of as paintings—seascapes, framed and set under glass. The rest of the place was Bare Studio; easel, tabaret, canvases neatly stacked against the wall. Visitors would always express their surprise that she "lived like that," and it would always annoy her. Just as it annoyed her that people assumed when she said "I'm a painter" that she meant once a week, for an hour, in the garden, wearing a pastel dress and a hat, she entertained callers and scribbled the flowers.

She had never, in fact, scribbled flowers.

Dallier, her first instructor in Paris, had eyed her severely the first time they'd met and said, *"Fais comme tu veux, mais pas de fleurs!"* (Do what you like, but no flowers!) And in five years of classes she had learned no flowers, but had taught herself her own vision and style. (Dallier had said, "I can never teach you, I can only be here to tell you when you've learned.")

For a moment now, walking to the sun-drenched kitchen, she remembered the time when she thought she'd never leave, when Paris had seemed so completely her home, and California had looked like the foreign shore. She'd had an apartment on Montparnasse in an ancient, gloomy building on a court. The apartment had been both a dream and a nightmare. The skylight, heavenly; the heat, nonexistent; and the rain—and there was nothing like a Paris rain—would bongo steadily against the windows. But if Paris was cold, it was also warm; at least to her. And she found herself in a small circle of friends—French, Egyptian, Indian, Dutch—people who didn't act as though they knew her before they'd met her, who didn't dismiss her as a "cheerleader type," because they didn't even know what a cheerleader was.

And then, Michel.

The telephone rang, jarring her back to the California sun, and she stood, undecisive, and then decided it was probably Clarissa, her mother's sister, asking if she couldn't hitch a ride tomorrow. Jennifer, of course, would give her the ride, but she didn't want to give her an hour on the phone. She just let it ring.

Fixing a sandwich, she thought about tomorrow. She'd visit her mother at, say, around three; first, pick up Clarissa, then pick up a gift. Candy or something. A bed jacket. A book. Flowers. Or probably all four. Things that people in hospitals liked. And she thought for a moment that the thing her mother liked best was the hospital. Being there soothed her. It hadn't been a serious operation. The doctor had said as much from the start. But still, her mother was fifty-seven, and the only dramas she looked forward to were bad ones, and now she was acting out *Woman in Pain,* a continuing drama, brought to you daily for seventeen years . . . Jennifer stopped. Unfair, she thought. I am being unfair. And besides, it was only sixteen years. The week of Jennifer's seventeenth birthday. . . .

"Jen? Where's your mother?" Her father's voice on the phone sounded strange. She put down her books on the hallway table.

"I don't know, Daddy. I just got home. We had this audition today after school. I just got—"

"Jen?"

"What?"

"Look . . . I'm . . . still on the road. It'll take me another hour to get home. Jen?" He sounded terrible now. "Jen? I was talking to your mother on the phone . . . a while ago . . . and she . . . Jen? Would you just go and see if she's home? Jen, oh, Jen, I'm sorry, oh, baby, I . . . Jen? Would you just go and see if she's home?"

Later, she remembered thinking he was angry, just flat out angry, but that wasn't fair. He'd been desperate, frustrated, angrily wanting to kick off the guilt, and Jennifer, sitting on the hard oak bench in the lime-colored disinfectant-smelling hall, had felt herself cursed for seeing both sides. There didn't seem to be a Wrong and a Right. There was only her father and her mother. Two tremendously unhappy people. And he had to get away from her or die. And she had to hold onto him or die. And he'd tried to get away and she'd tried to die.

Only, she hadn't locked the bathroom door, and Jennifer counted on seeing, forever, her mother lying in the red water, the red razor on the blue-striped bathmat and, God, oh, God, how awful, how frightening, how disgusting, how weak, to turn yourself into a floating red *thing,* into a piece of butchered flesh, to put your life into somebody's hands, so when they took away the hands . . .

He'd come back, of course. And they lived Quite Miserably Ever After. Because he never left again, never tried; he was beaten.

She brought her sandwich out to the easel and, standing barefoot in a salient of sunlight, chewed her lip and studied what she'd done. She stepped back slowly and, frowning, squinting, she tried to see it with a critic's eye.

"Jennifer Corley's pictures have a calm, a tranquillity that makes . . ."

Or: *"Jennifer Corley—a child prodigy of thirty-three—shows remarkable . . ."*

"Jennifer Corley, another talentless local dilettante, has managed to lower artistic standards . . ."

She turned and groaned as the telephone rang.

"Jennifer?"

"Yes?"

Her voice was the same. Catchy. Only slightly musical. He smiled, in a reflex. "There's no reason on God's earth for you to remember me, but . . . uh . . . this is Bob Morrison." He rubbed his jaw.

"From college?"

"Yeah."

"Well of course I remember you."

"Oh."

She laughed. "You sound disappointed."

He laughed. "It's just that you ruined my speech. I was ready to give you my vital statistics and distinguishing marks—adding, of course, a couple of inches, a lot of brawn, and a dueling scar. Listen, I . . . uh . . . happen to be in town on business, just overnight, and I wondered if you'd like to . . . I mean, if you were *free* to have dinner tonight." He fumbled a cigarette out of a pack, looked at it, and tossed it down on the bed. Outside the big hotel-room window he could hear the sound of splashing by the pool.

"Oh," she said. "Tonight. I'm sorry, I—"

"Right," he said quickly. "I didn't really—"

"How about late afternoon? I'd say come now, but I'm working at the moment and I've kind of got a deadline."

He sat on the bed, kicking off his shoes. "What do you do?"

She laughed. "I was just trying to decide. I mean, whether what I do is good or bad. I'm a painter."

"That's wonderful."

"You really think so?"

He laughed. "You sound disappointed."

She laughed.

"What time this afternoon?" he asked her. "Wait—I'd better tell you first that I've got a meeting at three-twenty-five."

"Three-twenty-*five*?"

"Right. I've been trying to dope it myself. How they arrived at that particular number. Anyway, I don't know how long it'll take."

"Well . . ." She paused. "Why don't you just . . . get here when you get here? I'll be home working anyway. At least until six. Then I've got to—"

"Fine," he cut her off quickly. "Just tell me where 'here' is, and then we'll be set."

"Got a pencil?"

"Yeah."

"One-nine-six-five-four Pacific Coast Highway. . . . You know how to get here?"

"No. And if you tell me, I'll feel like an ass when I get lost anyway, so just don't tell me."

She laughed. "You sound exactly the way you used to."

"Oh, no."

"That was a compliment."

95

"Oh." He scratched his head. "Yeah. Well ... I'll see you ... when I see you."

"Bob?"

"What?"

"Turn left half a mile from the Flying A sign."

IX

"Turn right," Mario said. "Soznick said turn right at Hillcrest."

"That wasn't Hillcrest. We're *on* Hillcrest. That was Santa Monica. We turn at Sunset."

"Oh."

Morrison turned to him now. "I'm navigator, you're bombardier. Why do you think they said three-twenty-five?"

"God only knows. But they said to be *prompt.*"

The rented car was a blue convertible, and Morrison leaned back, enjoying the ride, the feel of the wheel, the sun, the view.

The houses grew bigger as you traveled north. The closer to Sunset, the closer to heaven, he thought, and squinted at the homes up ahead. One had a lawn the size of a stadium; it banked downward from a central path. The

slopes of the bank were covered with ivy, and
the field at the bottom was a field of flowers.
No grass. Just flowers. Millions of pink and
fuchsia geraniums.

Soznick's house was on Sunset Boulevard.
Spanish stucco; a jolly pink giant. A nasty-
looking butler answered the door and then led
them through a black-and-white-tiled hallway
to a large glass door leading out to a pool.

It was, exactly, three-twenty-five.

They were sitting on the water: Soznick
and Foster. Sitting *on* it, in floating rubber
chairs. A floating rubber table with a phone
was between them. They were reading *Variety*. Morrison stared.

The papers went down, revealing two men,
a fat one and a bald one. Morrison blinked.
The glare from the water was practically
blinding. He could hardly see them. A blond, at
the shallow end, was feeding ... a duck?

The bald one said, "I'm Soznick. You Morrison?"

"Right. And this is Mario Marino."

Soznick nodded. "And this here's Foster." He
jerked his thumb toward the end of the pool.
"And one of those things over there is my
wife."

Neither the duck nor the woman looked up.

"So!" Soznick said. "Let's get right to it.
We heard your work and we think you can do
it." He laughed. "That rhymes. How's that?
Not bad," he answered himself. "However,"
he added, "I wanna tell you, it's a competition. We're tryin' out you and a few other
guys. Take a look at the script, do a couple
of songs, and then don't call us, and it's fifty-
fifty we won't call you. Got it?"

Morrison nodded.

"About money," Mario said.

"What money?" Foster looked up from *Variety* again. His several chests were hairy and brown. "It's a competition. Like a Pillsbury Bake-Off. You don't win the money till we've eaten the cake. You don't want to bake us a song, then don't." Foster looked back at *Variety* again.

Soznick said, "The script is up on the table." He jerked at a tile table on the side. On the table was a script and a television set.

Foster said, "Hey. It's three-thirty, Soznick."

Soznick said to Morrison, "And while you're up, would you turn the set on to CBS? *Guiding Light*. We don't like to miss it."

"That's *it*? That's *all*? That's the end of the meeting?"

"Sure. Unless you wanna stay and watch the show."

He left the car with Mario and took a taxi. And telling himself that he really wasn't going anyplace special, that he was simply having some coffee with a girl, an ordinary girl, or a girl who at least would seem ordinary now, in the light of mature, realistic appraisal, and telling himself she was probably married, this ordinary girl, because a girl so extraordinary wouldn't be single, and telling himself that even if she were, nothing would happen, not in a day, not, in fact, in a million years, he started looking through Soznick's script.

FADE IN ON

A CLOSE UP SHOT of a sleeping man. This is BILL CARTER, and his sleep is troubled. HE is pleasant-looking, dark, about thirty-five.

ANOTHER ANGLE (WIDER)
And we see a woman's hand, and

And the thing was good, it was really good. Soznick and Foster had actually chosen a beautiful script. The characters were real; they walked off the page and sat down beside you. You liked them; you cared; the emotions were real, not something made up out of typewriter ribbon and slick dialogue and writer's sweat. And, he thought, what a joy to score it.

He looked up and saw the gas-station sign. The letter A with a pair of wings. The Flying A.

"Make a left in another half-mile," he said, and then closed the script, staring at the shiny blue vinyl cover with the title stamped out in small gold letters: IF EVER I SEE YOU AGAIN.

He caught a glimpse of her, standing by an easel. Golden head; tan face, turning. And then she smiled, as he stood there, awkwardly, shifting his weight on the redwood porch. "Hey, come on in. I got a handful of yellow." And she rubbed her yellow-painted hand on a cloth as he opened the door.

And it was Time-Warp Time.

Her hair was the color of an alchemist's dreams, and it drifted to her shoulders in thick waves. Her eyes were that rare True Blue. He fumbled in his pocket till he found a cigarette, stuck it in his mouth, and forgot to light it.

So much, he thought, for time healing

all wounds. He hadn't thought of her at all in years. At least not much. Not till the day he'd run into Brookman. And then, when he had, it wasn't with any Romantic Hope. She belonged to the catalog of outgrown dreams. Her picture was there beside the ten-speed bike, the catcher's mitt, and the Purple Heart. He could even knock the lady because he'd tried her and she'd found him wanting, and he was much too old to play Romeo again. And still, his blood kept jumping around to the loony tune of Gene Kelly singing "Our Love Is Here to Stay."

He watched her as she laid down the paint-dotted rag and said: "You want coffee?" The music stopped. The moment passed. The Time Machine whirred and dropped him off at Now. He paid the driver and tipped him grandly.

"Fine," he said, and found a cigarette was stuck in his mouth, pulled it out, looked at it, rolled it around, stuck it back in, and forgot to light it.

"Nice house," he said, looking around.

She tilted her head and studied him now. "Do you really think so?" Her voice had a Tone; as though the question were a challenge.

He looked at her. "Yes. It's clean. Uncluttered. You can work here." He smiled. "And instead of *Kojak*, you can watch the sea."

Her smile seemed disproportionate now; he wondered whether she was laughing at him.

"I'll just be a minute," she said, and disappeared.

He lit the cigarette, and looked at her painting. He wasn't sure what she'd meant it to be, but he thought it looked like a wall with a window, the window looking out on an empty sky.

"Please don't feel you have to comment," she said.

He turned. She was standing with a round wooden tray: coffeepot, cups. For the first time he noticed what she was wearing—chinos and a workshirt, small silver heart on a chain around her neck. He wondered whose heart it was.

"I like it," he said. "Very much. It's . . . lonely."

She nodded. "Yes. That's what I meant."

"Are you?"

Her tawny eyebrows lifted. "No," she said. "Are you?"

"No."

"Cream?"

"Yes."

She poured the coffee. Then sat down beside him on the sailcloth couch. She smelled of sandalwood, turpentine, ocean. He couldn't look at her; he looked around the room. "Whose house is this?" he asked.

"Mine. All mine."

"*All* yours?"

She smiled. "Oh . . . no husband, if that's what you mean."

"I guess that's what I mean."

"How about you?"

"No husband, either."

"Mmm."

"I'm divorced."

"Kids?"

"Two. Boy and a girl."

"That's nice."

He was still looking around. "You have any more paintings?"

"Of course. But not here. I've got a show opening at a gallery on Monday. Park's, off La Cienega, if you're . . . Oh. I forgot. You said you won't be here."

"Yeah. I'd love to see it, but I'm leaving tomorrow. Davey—remember Davey Miller—"

"Of course—and I read about it in the paper. Carnegie Hall. I think it's terrific. Would you send him my regards?"

"Of course."

"You used to play piano yourself. Did you ever . . . go on to *do* something with it?"

He looked at her. "No. I sell plumbing insurance."

"What?" She giggled.

"Don't laugh. It's a very lucrative business. Our motto is, 'If you'd like to have a nickel for every time your drain clogs . . .' "

She nodded. "Saw the ad for it in *TV Guide*."

"You saw that."

"I saw that."

"You read that."

"I read that."

He suddenly laughed, throwing back his head. "And were you eating your heart out, thinking: Oh Lord, if I hadn't dropped him for Kenny Larkin—"

"Kenny *Larkin*?" Both of her hands flew up to her mouth, and she laughed through her fingers. "Now, *how* did you remember Kenny Larkin? Even *I'd* forgotten him."

"Yeah. Well, that's easy for *you* to say. But could Rhett forget Ashley? Could Cyrano forget Christian? And for that matter, could Tom forget Jerry? Man, that kid was the star of my nightmares. And I used to see the two of you, parked by the dorm in his little blue car, and I used to think: What the heck *does* she talk to him about?"

She rolled her eyes to the ceiling and laughed. "Nothing," she said, and lowered her eyes, and for just a second it seemed that she flushed.

He grinned at her slowly with his head to the side, thinking she didn't look silly when she flushed, and then she looked back at him, holding his look; and then she let it drop, so abruptly he could hear it crash. "More coffee?" she said.

"Yeah. Thanks."

"What I thought was," she said, handing him a cup, "I thought: That's terrific. He got what he wanted."

"And what had he wanted?"

"To show them," she said. "To get . . . to get even."

He smiled quickly. "And living well is the best revenge."

"Something like that."

He nodded. "Yeah . . ." And sipped the coffee.

"You enjoy it?" she asked.

"Living well? Oh, yeah."

"The work."

He shrugged. "Did once. Don't now. The answer's irrelevant."

"Is it?" She cocked her head at him, frowning. "Did you ever want to do anything else?"

"Sure." He shrugged. *"Wanting's* easy. But wanting something doesn't mean zip. The truth was—beyond all the cozy cop-outs—I just didn't want it enough to struggle. Why struggle? 'Meat' rhymes with 'treat,' and it's easy bread and easy success." He looked at her easel. "And Art is hard. It chews you up, and it usually doesn't give you anything back."

"Except for your soul."

"Oh. Soul. Don't have one." He grinned. "Sent it away with seventeen boxtops and a completed entry blank, *'I Like Wilkerson's Toothpaste Because . . .'*" He turned off the grin and looked at her levelly. "Does it make you happy, to work for your soul?"

She laughed. "Now, don't accuse me of being *happy.*"

The laughter was one of those too-bright bells, and he looked up sharply, stubbing his cigarette, and then nodded slowly. "So. You, too, have gotten kind of tough."

She shrugged. "Not exactly a girl you'd bring a rose to."

"Oh, I'd bring you roses. Ostentatious dozens. And how in the world did you remember *that*. Even *I'd* forgotten."

"Mmm." She put down her cup carefully and shrugged, carefully. "It was lovely," she said. "It made me cry."

"Cry?" He waited.

She was pouring coffee, not looking at him. He waited. She continued not looking at him. He waiting for a moment, saying nothing, then saying to himself: Okay, don't press it. She probably cried out of charitable pity. Or tears of laughter. "So tell me more about your work," he said quickly. "Is this your first show? Or your ninety-seventh? Or what?"

At least she looked at him again. "My sec-

ond. The first was in Paris," she said, leaning
back on the couch. "I lived there for . . . practically five years. And then . . . because it's a
small world, I met someone there who lived in
California. So then I moved back."

"And what happened to him?"

She shrugged. "He lived happily ever after."

"You never got married."

She shook her head. "And beyond, as you
said, all the cozy cop-outs, the truth is, I'm just
not the marrying kind."

"Uh-huh. And you think there's a 'marrying kind.' "

"Oh, yes." She smiled. *"You* were clearly
the marrying kind."

Frowning, he thought it over and shrugged.
"Well . . . I just wanted some woman to make
an honest man of me." He studied her. "And I
think you could have done it, too."

She shook her head. "No one makes anything out of anybody."

"Wrong. I think people can make each other happy."

"Or unhappy."

He nodded. "Or walnut pancakes."

"What?" She grinned again, biting her lip.

"My wife used to make me walnut pancakes. That was the height of her emotional
range. She bought it at the Sears appliance
center," he added. "The high emotional range.
It was self-cleaning."

Jennifer laughed. "You're nuts, you know?"

"Oh, no. I'm being profoundly profound.
I'm telling you What's Wrong with the Mod-
ern World: automatic, self-cleaning emotions,

and besides, the conversation was getting too serious, so I thought I'd break it up with a rotten pun."

She was looking at him now with a nice little smile, almost a nice little intimate smile, and he wanted to touch it, that particular smile, and he started to move, and the smile tightened, and she moved away quickly and looked at her watch.

"Would you like to go for a swim?" she said.

"Before we get in over our heads?"

She nodded slowly. "Something like that."

"I don't have trunks."

"I'll give you a pair. New. Unused. I bought them for someone, and I bought the wrong size."

He wanted to protest, but she was already halfway out of the room, and he let her go. She returned in a moment, tossing him a pair of navy briefs. "You can change in here. I'll change in the bedroom."

He nodded dumbly, feeling inanely awkward now as he stripped, and found himself standing naked, his body alert with misunderstanding. Wrong, he told it. Wrong room, wrong timing, wrong girl; and he put on the tight navy-blue briefs that were somebody else's wrong size.

The water was warm, and he followed her into it, watching her brown, supple body as she swam ahead of him, breaking into a fast crawl. A raft was tethered thirty feet out, and she said, "Some days the surf is so rough you can't get out there," but the water was calm and they swam to the raft, and pulled themselves onto it.

Morrison felt his heart beating fast, and he leaned back panting on the sun-hot wood.

"Ouch," he said. "Your raft's made of kindling wood."

She splashed it with water. "Better?" She smiled, and then lay back, closing her eyes in the yellow sun.

Leaning on his elbow, he studied her face, remembered lying beside her in bed and stroking her hair till a sun came up. With her eyes still closed, she lifted a hand and traveled it slowly down the side of his face; it reached his mouth, and he caught it, kissed it, tasting the salt.

"Oh, Jen," he said.

"Sssh."

He let out a guttural sound, and leaning forward, propped on his arms, feeling the sun's heat on his back, he tasted the salty heat of her mouth. Her arms went around him, cool and wet, and she pulled him closer, arching her back, making a soft sweet little sound.

And then suddenly she pulled away.

He caught her. "What are you *doing?*" he said.

She was shaking her head, biting her lip. Her eyes were open, wide and blue. And then she smiled and said very lightly, "Well . . . I guess I was kissing you, huh?"

He sighed. "Yeah. That's what it was."

Standing, she squinted into the sun. "You don't have a waterproof watch on, do you?"

"Nope. But I know what time it is, Jen."

It was almost six when they got to the house. He lit a cigarette, and asked if he could possibly use her phone to call for a cab. She said she'd drive him. He said, "Oh, no."

"Don't be silly. I'm going in that direction. Look. Just wait while I throw on some clothes."

Dressed, he waited, pacing the room, then walked to the porch and stared at the sea. It was already pulling away from the shore, leaving a dark ring on the sand. He stubbed the cigarette and kicked it away.

Once again she'd afflicted him—that was the word, there was no other word he could think of that fit. He wanted to return to his normal fine ironic spirit, to get on top of it, make it a joke, but there was no audience out here to laugh, except for the ocean, which didn't give a damn.

He wanted her.

In the same way he'd wanted her thirteen unlucky years ago, and in a way he'd never wanted anyone else. And she was still as quixotic, as warm-cool, push-pull, near-far as she'd ever been. And he had to ask himself, once again, if he wasn't simply asking for trouble, and if Jennifer wasn't, after all, simply a girl who liked to create it.

But he couldn't, or maybe wouldn't, believe it. He figured now as he'd figured then, that Jennifer Corley was something special. Complicated (God only knew), but a girl who wanted and needed love, and more than that, a girl who gave it—naturally, easily, and *then* she pulled back.

Leaning now on the redwood rail, he cautioned himself to be careful, smart. On the ride into town, he'd have to be cool—casual, laid-back, California-cool. . . .

"Ready?" she said. She was wearing a pale yellow silk blouse with white linen pants and a white sweater. The car keys jingled in her hand.

He nodded. "Yeah. Ready," he said.

6:15

Hey you old sonofagun. I'm sitting here, being stood up in the bar, and I happen to hear your name being paged. If you're back before 7, I'll buy you a drink. I haven't changed at all in the last 13 years. I still look like a guy who'd be stood up for drinks.

It was written on a doctor's prescription blank, that said CHARLES WILLIAMS, M.D. at the top.

Morrison looked at the lobby clock. Ten of seven. He walked to the bar, a room that was neither quiet nor dim, a room full of plants and wine-colored carpet, and things on-the-rocks, and people who looked like celebrities, or were trying to look like celebrities, or were trying to look *at* them. Someone who looked like Chad Everett was signing an autograph for someone who looked like Johnny Carson. Or maybe, he thought, it was the other way around. It was hard to tell.

Charlie Williams did not look like a guy who'd be stood up for drinks. He was tan, handsome, and disgustingly fit.

"Tennis," he said. "Tennis and swimming."

Morrison ordered a scotch on the rocks.

"And very little booze," Williams added. "And I quit smoking."

Morrison quickly lit up a smoke. "Nine out

of ten doctors," he said, "are terribly boring. You know that, Charlie?"

Williams grinned. "So are nine out of ten commercials, but yours are terrific."

"Yeah. Cheers." Morrison drank.

"All things considered, you look pretty good."

Morrison looked at him, over the glass. "And just what things are we considering, Charlie?"

"Age, life-style, medical history. Yeah. I'd say you look pretty good. . . . But I bet you haven't had a checkup in years."

Morrison squinted down at his glass, and remained squinting for a long moment. Something here was as cute as a snake, as subtle as a hammer, and as much of a coincidence as Christmas always falling on December 25.

And then he looked up and saw Mario there, standing in the doorway. He waved him over and made introductions.

Mario said, "Didn't catch the name."

"Williams," Williams announced. "Charlie."

"Doctor," Morrison said, "M.D. Stands for Magnificently Devious, right?"

Nobody knew what he was talking about.

Mario said he'd spent the afternoon swimming.

Morrison said he'd spent the afternoon punting.

Williams said he'd spent the afternoon working, that sometimes he even worked evenings too, and that he'd really be happy to give Morrison a checkup, adding that his office was right down the block.

Warner, Morrison thought, Warner. Warner must have set up this cute little trap. Morrison looked up, smiled very nicely, and said, "Listen, doctor. Get off my case."

Williams shrugged. "Tell Warner I tried."

"I'll do that. And besides, I'm not free tonight. I got a heavy date with a foxy script. If I play my cards right, I can take it to bed."

Morrison woke with the script on his bed, and sunshine blasting in through the drapes. It was eight-thirty. The flight was at noon. He looked at the script, said, "Kid, you were great," and, rolling over, he picked up the phone and ordered a huge room-service breakfast.

Lighting his first cigarette of the day, he walked to the window and opened the drapes. The room was up on the fifth floor, and, leaning over its balcony rail, he could see the impossibly turquoise pool. There were girls at the pool; stunning; sunning. There were tables with orange-and-white umbrellas, and men at the tables; eating; meeting; cheating; moguling; ogling the girls at the pool. There were white trellises, red bougainvilleas, green palm trees, and blue sky. It looked like a commercial, Morrison thought. And he felt like the only real person in the middle of a silly television world.

When the breakfast arrived—a grapefruit the size of a basketball, eggs, bacon, toast, and coffee in a silver pot—he brought the tray to the balcony table and, eating, thought about what he should do: go down to the pool, swim, relax.

Which had nothing to do with what he would do.

By nine-thirty, with his coat and his duffel

bag over his arm, he was facing the desk clerk, scrawling a note.

"For Mario Marino," he said to the clerk, handed him the note, and then tipped the doorman to get him a cab.

X

Park's Gallery was a two-story Spanish stucco building with a red tile roof and arched windows, some of which gave onto a tiled court. A small fountain played in the court, watering the water from a large bronze elephant's mouth.

Morrison put his bag on the floor, his coat on a chair, and cleared his throat.

The salesgirl sitting at the desk, he thought, looked fairly efficient for California; she wasn't tan and her feet weren't bare. She looked up slowly from her morning cruller, through granny glasses and dazzling sun.

"Can I help you?"

He nodded. "You have some paintings of Jennifer Corley's?"

"Yes. We're setting them up tomorrow."

"Yes. But you have them here today."

"Yes. But the show doesn't start till Monday."

Yes, he told her, he knew about that, but explained that he couldn't come back on Monday, and managed to pry out the information that the paintings were stored in a room upstairs. "A closet, really, and Mr. Park doesn't like—"

"Where in he?"

"Who?"

"Mr. Park."

"In Catalina."

"Uh-huh?" Morrison tilted his head.

The girl tilted hers. "You just browsing, or you really serious?"

"I'm so serious it scares me," he said.

"Huh?"

"I'll undoubtedly buy one," he said. "I'll leave my address. You can air-ship it to me at the end of the show. How long does it last, by the way?"

"Till Christmas," she said, getting up from the desk.

She led him up a flight of red-tiled stairs, and into a nine-by-eleven room with vertical shelving lining the walls. "Those." She pointed. "Right side, bottom. From there to there." Frowning, she looked at him, shifting her weight. "I guess they're too big to steal," she said, but then cast an eye at the upper shelves.

"You can frisk me when I leave," he suggested.

She shrugged. "I just might do that," she said, and left.

There were twenty paintings. He studied them intently for almost an hour, trying to read them, he finally realized, as though they were Jennifer Corley's palm, or a set of ambiguous tarot cards that were somehow reporting his own fate.

They were abstract paintings, large and bold. Blocks of color, looming like walls; lines reaching out, struggling tensely to meet other lines, and always missing. The paintings were strong.

One of them seemed in a different mood, and from Morrison's mood; he saw it as a door. A dark door in a dark room, but a light was shining around the cracks, as though once the door were finally opened, the view would be one of dazzling light.

"Number seventeen," he said at the desk.

The girl looked it up on a typewritten sheet. *"Door to the Nightgarden,* that one's called."

He was folding the receipt when the door opened, and he turned, and Jennifer saw him and smiled. He hastily shoved the receipt in his pocket and said, "What are *you* doing here? I thought you said you had a plane to catch."

Quickly she said, "But I wanted to look at a friend's paintings before I left town. Which is lovely of me. Thank you, Jennifer."

He smiled. She was wearing last night's clothes. The yellow shirt and the white pants, and he knew what it meant. "You're wonderful, Jen. The work is superb. But you have to go, or you'll miss your plane."

"You'll drive me," she said.

"I've got work to do here."

"Yes. But you'd *like* to drive me." She smiled. "Really." Some hair tipped over her eyes, and she pushed it back with a brisk hand.

"All right," he said, reluctantly though.

Bending, he picked up his coat and his bag and followed her out into yellow heat.

"I bet it's cold in New York," she said.

They were on the freeway; the wind was fooling around with her hair, fanning it around like yellow flames.

He nodded. "Yeah. I bet," he said, and remembered how much she hated the cold. He watched her profile, lit by the sun. He could think of nothing unimportant to say, so he said nothing for a long time.

"I forgot to ask you," she said.

"What?"

"What kind of business you were out here on."

He told her, repeating the poolside interview, elaborating on it, till he had her laughing so hard she said: "Stop! I can't drive and laugh at the same time."

He said: "So pull over and let me drive."

She said: "You like to be in the driver's seat, don't you?"

He said: "So do you."

She nodded. "You're right. That way I always know where I'm going."

"Around in circles."

She looked at him sharply, but then, to his surprise, she nodded again. "Yes. I guess. We all travel in limited circles, don't we?"

He let it go. Their relationship was a closed circle. He lit a cigarette, and watched the scenery: sun and palms and fast-driven cars. Leaning over, he turned on the radio. "Fair and eighty degrees," it said. And the sign to the airport flashed overhead.

"Bob?"

He turned. She was watching the road.

"I hope you're not sorry you called me," she said. "Because . . . I—"

"No." He laughed suddenly, tossing his cigarette out the window. "It seems to me we've already played this scene. And why should I be sorry? I got a cup of coffee, a kiss, and a swim. What more could a reasonable man expect?"

She looked at him slowly. "I'm glad," she said. "Because I . . . I really like you . . ."

"I'm nice," he said.

"You are," she said. "And I hope we can be friends." She smiled. "I was always sorry we couldn't be friends. I used to look at you, too, you know. With Davey and Warner and Laura. . . . And you always looked as though . . . you were having a very good time. As though you *had* something."

"Friendship," he said.

"That's an art," she said.

"Eleven-thirty-five," the radio said.

"Time to go," he said.

"I hope you get to do the movie," she said.

"Yeah. And good luck on your show," he said.

He grabbed his bag from the back seat, and, turning, he found her lips close to his. "Don't start," he told them. "Just say good-bye."

She looked at him, nodding, and said, "Good night."

Counterpoint

XI

They celebrated Davey's concert perfor-
mance till four in the morning, starting at the
Russian Tea Room, right down the block from
Carnegie Hall, starting with champagne and
Russian caviar, and continuing with champagne and chili at Clark's, and ending up back
at Davey's apartment, an inner circle of five
people, "diehards," Davey said, "drinkhards,"
Warner said, and somebody said they ought to
check the reviews, and Morrison, quite re-
markably drunk, had walked about seven
blocks for a paper, returning up the four
flights of stairs to proclaim, "brilliant," "amazing," "tender," "rare," and then added he'd
been reading a holiday ad for a sirloin special
at the A&P.

Sunday he slept, waking when the clock said
6:31, and he moaned, thinking it was much

too early, and then realized it was 6:31 *P.M.*, and the children were already eating supper.

"What's that," he said, drinking his orange juice slowly and eyeing their plates.

"Turkey hash," Johnathan said.

"With cream sauce," Amy added, smiling.

"Oh," he said, feeling not-very-well.

"Where are you going, Daddy?"

"To sleep."

That was Sunday.

Monday, at a meeting on Mr. Chunky, the men at Chalmers' agency announced they'd decided to test some "different approaches." Three, in fact. Three different ways of selling the dog food. They'd test them in each of three small cities, compare the results, and go with the winner for the national pitch.

Morrison spent Monday locked in his workroom with a plastic bag full of large extruded diamond-shaped chunks, and came up with "Diamonds Are a Dog's Best Friend." To his dismay, he found himself pleased with the line.

That was Monday.

Tuesday at noon he walked to the corner of Fifth and Forty-second, to the big green out-of-town-newspaper stand, and picked up a copy of the L.A. *Times*. Arriving early at A&R Sound, he sat in the control booth and opened the paper to the section on "Arts" and:

THE LYRIC ABSTRACTION OF
JENNIFER CORLEY

Rarely do you leave a gallery humming the paintings, but when you leave Park's Gallery, don't be surprised if you find yourself singing, for instance, *Surfsong*, or *Morning #128*. These, among others of

Ms. Corley's works, demonstrate a new
and imaginative vision—line, as lyric;
shape, as song . . .

He looked up, discovering Warner wincing,
muttering something about Morrison's need-
ing his head, as well as everything else, exam-
ined.

They discussed it over air hockey later that
day.

"Nasty," Warner said, "or very nasty. She's
one or the other"—he lobbed—"or both. She's
a bitch and a tease," he elaborated crisply,
"and I hope all the fairy tales had it down right
and she winds up a scrawny, lonely old maid.
And besides—"

"She's in love with somebody else. Or she
just doesn't find me fatally attractive. And besides, what difference does it possibly make? I
get to California maybe two times a decade."

"Yeah? What about if you do this movie."

"It's a post-score job. When the film's in
the can, I can work with it here."

"Well . . . that doesn't make her less nasty,"
Warner said.

"You're wrong."

"And you're horny. That's all. And that's
game," Warner said. "You owe me a nickel.
Pay."

And Morrison tossed him a coin. "Here, kid,
Get lost."

Tuesday, he paced until four A.M., scribbling
notes, scrawling lyrics, writing songs, and
then tearing them up. They were all "compe-
tent," all "good," but his inner critic had said
"not great." It hadn't been until Thursday
morning, at 5:14 by the digital clock, that

he'd looked at his scribbles and thought: Okay. I think you did it. A possible win.

And now the day was intruding again. A morning session for Diet-Delish; a three-o'clock meeting with Almond Crunch. He sat in the taxi with Warner at his side and looked at his watch. 1:15. They'd stopped for a light, and outside the window some kids were climbing a three-foot mountain of hard, lumpy, graying snow, surrounded by a mountain of bagged garbage. Morrison looked at it bleakly for a while, then opened his briefcase and took out the script.

On page 38, the girl shook her head and said:

(*softly*)
Billy . . . it just won't work. We're
too different.

CARTER
To what? To love each other?

ANNABELLE
No. To make it work.

CARTER
(grimly)
If love doesn't work, then nothing does.

CLOSE ON ANNABELLE
Annabelle shrugs.

REVERSE (CARTER)
He shakes his head, looks to the side.

HIS POINT OF VIEW
The battered truck, parked on the path.

HOLD

As Carter enters the frame, alone. HE opens the door of the truck, looks up slowly.

HIS POINT OF VIEW

Annabelle turns, enters the house.

MEDIUM SHOT

Carter, slamming the door of the truck. He turns the ignition. And then

DISSOLVE

He's driving into an orange sunrise. MUSIC plays. The lyrics should capture Carter's mood.

Morrison pulled out a ball-point pen and wrote:

> *lonely highways that stretch out*
> *to nowhere*
> *and I'm never turning for home.*
> *The*

"We're home, kid." Warner's voice broke the thought. The cab had stopped at their office building. "The office awaits. And so, by the way, does Hamilton Rush."

"Oh God. In the office?" Morrison said.

"Not in ours. He's waiting in his. By the red phone. He wants you to call."

Morrison shoved the script in his briefcase as Warner paid and got out of the cab.

They entered the small marble lobby.

"He's got a drain cleaner," Warner was saying. "A drain-cleaner *crisis*, I think was the word."

Morrison entered the elevator now. Warner pushed 7. The doors closed. Morrison felt he was locked in a cage. Or a very small execution chamber, with the cyanide pellet about to be dropped. He wasn't finding it easy to breathe.

The doors opened up on the seventh floor, on a wall with the Morrison Music logo. The M's were made out of triplet notes.

♫ORRISON ♫USIC

He glared at the sign, and Anne, the receptionist, who sat in front of it, said, "Are you mad at me, Bob?"

"Sorry. No. I was just looking over that Mickey Mouse sign. It looks like Mickey Mouse," he said to Warner. "Little tiny black-mittened hands." He tossed his coat on the wooden tree and, turning, walked down the narrow hall.

"Am I catching tiny black-mittened vibes?" Warner had followed him into his office, and stood now, watching as Morrison sat.

Morrison sat there, tapping a ball-point pen on the desk. It flashed on him now that Major Decisions were never really decisions at all. They were things that more or less happened to you. "Yeah," he said, looking at Warner. "And I think it's put-up-or-shut-up time, and I just decided I can't put up. I want to get out of the business, Warner. I'll finish the stuff that's already in, but I won't take on any new assignments. I think we can—"

"Careful." Warner sat down. "You don't have the Hollywood thing in the lock-up."

"I know. But I feel like *I'm* in the lock-up. Look, you can keep—"

"Forget about me. What about you? If you don't get the movie, what'll you do?"

"Something."

"Yeah? *What* 'something'? You're a song-writer, man. And you want to write songs, you got three ways to go. Fame, the poorhouse, or Madison Avenue. That's all there is, and there ain't no more, and I'm here to tell you the Terrible Truth. There reaches a point where you can't change your life. You're too far into it, too far gone. Your eggs are all sitting in one small basket, and all your experience locks you in, and you're much too old to be a fireman now, and it's much too late for computer school, and you'd absolutely totally *hate* being broke."

Morrison nodded. "I'd hate being broke."

Warner nodded. "So try for Fame, but keep your ace in the hole, your hat in the ring, and your name on the door."

Morrison swiveled around in his chair. Leaning his elbows on the desk, he pushed up his glasses and knuckled his eyes. It was true, he thought. It was really true. He was really stranded in his own life. There was alimony and Elsa to pay. There was school tuition for private schools, and after that, there'd be college tuition, and in between there'd be orthodontia and music lessons and summer camp. And, forgetting that, there was Morrison's limited listing of skills. He could tie his shoes; he could fry an egg. He could play the piano and lead a band. Which could lead him back into dingy nightclubs, summer theaters, and high-school proms. Because—and here was the nasty thought—because he was *not* a brilliant pianist. Davey Miller he'd never be. Peter Duchin he'd never be. Or Victor Borge, or Bobby Short . . .

"Could I rent a cape and be Liberace?"

"What?"

"Never mind. Leave my name on the door. If I flunk in the flickers, I'm sentenced to life."

Frowning, Warner stood up to go. He fingered his beard and shifted his weight. "Hey, look, man, I don't want to sound like the warden. Bob, if—"

"You sound like a sensible man. I'll finish the Wirtz and the Almond Crunch and then I'll go 'way and work on my score. They want the demo on December eighth."

"You'll give 'em a winner."

"Five winners. I gotta have five. Five songs. That's what they want."

"One, five. What's the difference?"

"Four," Morrison said. "Good-bye."

It rained, a soft, fat rain that chilled, on the second day, into sleet. On the third day, Sunday, the rain didn't rest; it was hard and fast and pinged like pebbles against the panes.

Jennifer stood at the picture window watching the gray redundant sea. Tom was still lying asleep in the bedroom, while the television set was blatting the news.

It was raining; that was the news.

Impatient, she turned away from the window and, passing the still-unfinished canvas, went to the kitchen and stood at the sink.

A copy of the Sunday New York *Times* sat,

fat, on the vinyl counter, splats of dried-up rain on its face. Tom had arrived with it late last night, so in case she'd somehow forgotten the date, the paper would be there to spell it all out.

It was Sunday; day of rest and reckoning. And, uncoincidentally, the day of his birthday.

She opened a can of Hills Brothers coffee and studied the Indian swami on the can. "Swami" meant "lord and master" in Hindu, and she looked at the harmless face on the can, with the yellow bandanna wrapped on its head, and she pictured Tom with a yellow bandanna wrapped on his head. Swami: master; owner; prince.

It had started at the gallery Monday night— a party launching the beginning of her show. And he'd left the party with somebody else; an obvious dark-eyed Swedish blond. It was not surprising, and not the first time, and certainly within the rules of the game. The rules being, both could "see other people"—only, Tom saw his "other people" in bedrooms, and Jennifer (a secret she did not confide) only saw hers in restaurants and bars.

But the obvious way he'd done it had bothered her (embarrassed her, angered her), and Wednesday she'd drummed up a nice little fight. They'd met for drinks and he'd looked at her over his glass, darkly, and said, "Listen, lady, who are *you* to talk?"

Frowning, she said she didn't know what he meant.

"I came back to get my watch on Friday."

Puzzled, she frowned. "You didn't," she said, "I brought it to you at—"

"Yeah. I left it. I didn't want you to know I'd been there. Or know that I'd seen you. Out on the raft."

"Oh." She shrugged, stirring her drink. On the verge of assuring him *that* was nothing, an old friend from college, nothing at all, she was suddenly fully and consciously aware that it was not nothing, that it absolutely was not nothing at all, that she'd felt for a moment she was drowning out there, that his arms around her were pulling her down into some deep terrible bottomless ocean, and she'd had to struggle, to surface, to breathe.

"It was nothing," she said. "An old friend from school, though I shouldn't reassure you. . . ."

He smiled at her then, stirring his coffee. "Listen," he said, "I am not made of rock. I was jealous. I didn't think I would be, you know? But I was. And yesterday I really kicked it around." He looked at her now, his brown eyes solemn. "It's my birthday next week," he said. "Four-Oh. And I suddenly started to think about time. It's passing, you know?" He shrugged. "And I started to think about us. Like, why don't we play it straight with each other? I mean, I'm forty and you're thirty-three, and we've never made commitments to anyone, have we? And maybe we can't. But maybe we should try. So I wonder if we ought to start living together. Just see how it goes, you know what I mean? But I think we either ought to tie it or tear it. I mean, I think we ought to do it or split."

She stared at him. The man who'd once carefully told her, "The only thing I want you to give me is space." At forty, it seemed the spaceman was grounded. Suddenly, abruptly; like Cinderella, at the stroke of the clock.

"Just think it over," he said to her slowly. "Give me your answer for a birthday present. That's ten more days."

She'd told him she would.

But the week had been crowded and she hadn't really thought, beyond being fairly certain that the answer was no. But she'd try to convince him there wasn't much difference between living together and what they had now. And just as certainly, he'd tell her there was, that the difference was "commitment." (A terrible word; they "committed" people to institutions.)

She opened the coffee pot, finding it loaded with yesterday's grounds. The trashcan was full, so she reached for the paper, looking for a section she wouldn't want to read. *Real Estate*. (He'd want it.) *Sports*. (He'd kill her.) *Business*. (He'd want it.) But the back of it was ads, filled with "Business Opportunities in Southern New Jersey," and she opened the section to tear out a page.

Morrison looked at her, smiling vaguely, and for just a moment she thought she'd gone nuts. But then she saw it was the advertising column (no mystical haunting, no lunatic lapse). He was wearing a slightly bemused expression, as though having the photograph taken was perplexing, and as soon as it was over, he was going to demand an explanation from himself.

JINGLE JANGLE, the headline read.

> The only difference between a Hollywood movie and a TV commercial is 104 minutes and 32 seconds.
> Maybe.

If Ever I See You Again

Testing that "maybe" is Robert Morrison, creator of Mad Ave.'s top ten hits, who is now competing (against Richard Arden, who scored *Pacific* and *Tower of Hell,* and Robert Langley, of *Dreamboat,* and *Love Is a Mockingbird* fame) for the assignment of scoring a Hollywood flick, Columbia's *If Ever I See You Again.*

Sitting in his Park Avenue apartment, in a chair that looks like a catcher's mitt, with a couple of kids running in and out, a telephone ringing, a vacuum cleaner buzzing in the room next door, and a jackhammer blasting on the street below, he tells me only that he hopes he can do it.

I tell him, "That's not exactly Hollywood hype."

He grins. "That's because I'm not a Hollywood type." He winces at the rhyme, but then goes on to tell me that he's just lost a round "in the battle of the coasts." The producers wanted him to work in California.

"Why don't you want to work in California."

"It's *impossible* to work in California. *Nobody* works in California. The place just wasn't *designed* for work." He lights a cigarette. "The whole state is shaped like a lounge chair. You ever *notice* that? Look at a map."

"You don't like to work in a lounge-chair state."

"I like to work in a state of nervous exhaustion. I like New York."

"But the movie's a love story set in California."

"So? And *Star Wars* was set out in space. You don't have to live what you're writing, you know. If I had to fall in love with a Californian to score this movie . . ."

He suddenly stops. "I'd qualify." He laughs.
"I'd win hands down."

"But you lost the battle."

"Oh, yeah," he says. "So I guess I'll be
out there for a couple of weeks."

"And when . . ."

"Jen?"

She turned. Tom was standing there, barefoot, yawning in the doorway. He coughed,
stretched, yawning again.

"Happy birthday," she said.

XII

He worked. He did not call her. He had
meetings with Soznick and Foster. Soznick
gave him lyric ideas. ("How about, 'Once in
love with Annabelle, always in love with Annabelle'?") Foster gave him musical ideas.
("Drums. I like drums. Plenty of drums.") He
watched three episodes of *Guiding Light*. Mrs.
Soznick was named LaVerne. The duck was
named Shirley. That was that.

He worked. He did not call her. He had lunch
at the Beverly Hills Hotel and saw Catherine
Deneuve in the Polo Lounge. He did not call her.
He took a walk down Beverly Drive and
stopped for a soda at Wil Wright's and stared
at the phone booth in the back of the shop.
And did not call her. He worked in a small
room at Columbia. The room had a baby grand
and a phone. He had it removed.

He went for a drive. He drove out to Santa

Monica Bay. It was near Malibu. He didn't go nearer. He left the car and walked on the beach. He told himself he was not in love. That a grown-up person was not in love with someone he'd been with for only an hour after thirteen years. Or even with someone he'd been with for two hours and twenty-five minutes, not counting the ride to the airport. He told himself she was not that special, not that wonderful, not that fine. He told himself that she wasn't as beautiful as she'd been, that she wasn't that clever, that she was, above all, inconvenient at this time, that he had work to do, and if there were any romantic ideas in his head, he could put them to better use in a song. He went back to his hotel room and wrote her a song. He put everything he felt about her in the song, all the emotion, confusion, amazement, the amazement of feeling emotion, the confusion of feeling amazed; it was not a clever song, there were no astonishing rhymes in it, no flashy triplets, nothing as facile or easy as that; it was full of hard simplicity. He called it "Annabelle," because that was the name of the girl in the film, but the name Annabelle scanned the way Jennifer did, and he'd always know it was Jennifer's song. And he did not call her.

She was glad he hadn't called. According to the paper, he'd been due to arrive on December 1. And if he'd called, she would have refused to see him. So it was just as well that he hadn't called.

Because she'd promised Tom; promised she'd move in with him in time for Christmas; promised she'd give it an honest try.

And she'd never made anyone a promise before, because she knew her sense of honor would force her to keep it. And now she was forced into keeping her promise—or accepting that she really had no sense of honor.

She remained uncertain as to *why* she'd promised. It might have had something to do with a challenge; or a catcall—the famous pop-psych jeer that people who "couldn't commit" themselves were somehow defective. And as Tom had said: "You're thirty-three." So at thirty-three, she would try commitment. And then, at least, she could say, "I tried." And maybe she'd succeed.

One night, painting, almost at dawn, an unwelcome thought had burst through her mind that she'd somehow locked herself into Tom exactly and only as a way of protecting herself from Bob. But she'd realized quickly that that was absurd. Morrison was a nice man; that was all. And if she felt for him . . . some kind of physical attraction, that's all that it was: a physical attraction.

A strong one, she conceded. And her mind went back to the first time. And it had been the first time. She'd still been a virgin when she'd slept with him in college. She wondered if he'd known that; he probably hadn't. Everyone assumed she'd been sleeping with Kenny, and Kenny had probably bragged that she was. And later, she did. But it hadn't been the same. It hadn't been that same feeling of . . . drowning. . . .

The telephone rang.

It was probably Tom.

He'd lain quite still on the patio chaise, staring at the phone on the white metal table, staring at his own sun-browned arm, as though it were somebody else's arm, the arm of a remote, sun-browned stranger. And he'd watched, almost idly, as the stranger's arm had reached for the phone, and his fingers had dialed the numbers.

"Where are you?" she asked.

"San Diego," he said, for no particular reason.

"What are you doing in San Diego?"

"What are you doing in Malibu?"

"Painting."

"Oh."

"Are you drunk?" she said.

"A little."

"Oh."

He shifted the phone in his hand. In front of him a green palm tree hissed, in a sudden gusting of palmy breeze. "What are you doing tomorrow?" he said.

"Painting."

"Oh." He nodded slowly. "Are you painting lyrically?"

"What?"

"Lyrically. I read that you painted lyrically."

"You read that?"

"I read that. And I thought if you were still painting lyrically, you might come over and paint my lyrics."

"Are you very drunk?"

"No. Not very. I'm inviting you to come to a recording session."

"The songs from the film?"

"Yeah. They're done. In fact, we're recording tonight in L.A. Place called E&M on Sunset. Seven o'clock. I figured, after, you could take me to dinner."

137

"Oh."

Silence.

He nodded. "Sounds like I figured wrong."

"It's just that I . . . have to work."

"Sure."

"You understand."

"Sure." And he knew he should say good-bye and hang up the phone. But the suntanned hand kept holding it tight.

"You . . ." she said.

"Yes?"

"You bought one of my paintings."

"Yes. . . . Wasn't I supposed to?"

"Yes . . . No . . . I mean, I would have liked to have given it to you."

From his chair he had a head-on view of the pool. A blond in an orange satin suit was posing, arched, on the diving board. She stayed, in perfect Olympic position, while a fat man snapped her picture below, and then, smiling, she turned and walked down the ladder. He said: "You don't owe me anything, Jen."

She said nothing.

His hand kept holding onto the phone.

Finally she said: "Well . . . listen . . . good luck with the movie. I hope you win."

"Yeah," he said. "So do I. Good-bye." And the hand let go of the phone before she could answer.

Warner and Mario were sitting at one of the poolside tables under one of the orange-and-white umbrellas. Mario had flown out three days before to book the talent for the demo session. Warner had come along for the ride. And the sun. In three days Warner had turned to the color of expensive English riding boots.

"Sorry." Morrison slid to his chair. "We've cast all the parts in the pirate movie, but shave off the beard and come back tomorrow and we'll see if we can use you in *Orphans of the Storm*."

"What are you drinking?" Mario said.

"Tequila."

"Great."

"It's very Hollywood," Morrison said. "Very Mexican. You notice how everyone out here loves everything Mexican except the Mexicans?"

"What?"

"He's saying," Warner explained, "that they don't love Mexicans. Social Comment for the afternoon." He turned to Morrison. "How are you feeling?"

"Mexican." Morrison smiled exquisitely.

"Wonderful." Warner shook his head. "So you called her."

"Who?"

"Your Mexicali rose."

"Like hell. I was just calling for the time. Sometimes I don't know what time it is, so I call for the time. At the tone the time will be three-twenty-eight and forty-two seconds. Bong."

"Would you like some coffee?"

"No. I think I want to watch *Guiding Light*. I want to know if Ed really died in the car crash and if Madge soaked any more hands in Palmolive."

Warner and Mario exchanged a look. Warner nodded.

Morrison squinted. "What?" he said.

"While you're in such a mellow mood"—Mario was scratching the back of his neck—"we've got a little proposition to make."

"Shoot."

"We don't have a piano player yet."

Morrison sobered. "Tell me that's a lie."

"That's the truth."

"Then lie to me and tell me it's a lie."

Warner shook his head. "It's the level truth. And you know how important the piano part is."

"I *know* how important the piano part is. I *wrote* how important the piano part is. So why the hell aren't you guys on the phone?"

"That's the little proposition we've got." Mario smiled. "I have in my possession a list of names and telephone numbers that I will not call—"

"That you will *not* call?"

"Unless," Warner said, "you proceed immediately to two-twenty-one South Reeves drive and let Charlie Williams give you a checkup."

"You devious creep!" Morrison glared. "That's blackmail!"

"Right," Warner smiled. "But it's very Hollywood. Very Mexican. In fact, it's known as a Mexican standoff."

"I'm not sick," Morrison said. "So you can get that canary-eating grin off your face."

"Shut up and say 'Aaah,'" Williams commanded.

"I can't shut up and say 'Aaah.' I can either shut up *or* say 'Aaah,' but I can't—"

The tongue depressor silenced all sound.

"Your throat looks fine," Williams announced.

"Yeah? Well, that's more than I can say for your nostrils. They've got nasty black hairs in them, you know that, Charlie?"

"Lie back on the table."

"I'll get you for this."

The stethoscope, cold, went down on his chest. Morrison felt himself holding his breath.

"Breathe naturally," Williams said, looking up sharply. "Through your nose. I want your mouth to be shut."

Morrison let his mouth remain shut. Because he was scared. Because of those ax blows of pain in his chest. Because he'd listened to his heart going *boom* after doing practically nothing at all. Because he'd been smoking like a dragon. "Well?" he said.

Williams shrugged. "I've heard better. It's a little irregular."

"Sure. My heart beats *dum*-da-da-dum. Just like a *drum*-da-da-da-dum. It's truth in advertising. The FCC made me swear out a—"

"Sit up."

Morrison sat.

The stethoscope went down again.

Williams listened. He pulled away, pulling the stethoscope out of his ears. "I'll tell you one thing. You're *tight* as a drum. You always this tense?"

"I got a big recording session tonight."

"Answer the question. You always this tense?"

"No. Yes. About half the time."

"And you smoke . . . ?"

141

"Too much."

"And you drink?"

"Not much. About three times a year I tie something on, but that's it."

"And you exercise?"

"Waving my arms."

"What does that mean?"

"Conducting orchestras, hailing taxis. Well ... and sometimes I walk a lot."

"Uh-huh." Williams was opening a cabinet, pulling out a small black leather case. He opened the case. He pulled out some little gizmos with wires.

"What the hell are those?"

"What do they look like?"

"They look like a set of extra nipples."

"Exactly. So I'll just pin them on your chest." And Williams started to do just that.

"What the—?"

"An electrocardiogram. If you'd been to a doctor in the last ten years, you wouldn't be asking such dumb questions."

"Oh, swell. How long is this thing gonna take? Charlie, I have to *leave* here any minute. And that's no bull. I really have to go and conduct a session."

"So you'll leave here with eight extra nipples."

"Funny. You got wires five miles long? Because the studio's in—"

"Bob. It's a portable machine. You leave this stuff on for twenty-four hours. Do everything you'd do ordinarily. Conduct, walk, climb stairs, make bad jokes, have sex—"

"Is that an order?"

Williams grinned. "Do the best you can. I

want to see what happens when you're under stress."

"Stress I can promise you."

Williams just nodded. "Drop the machine off tomorrow. I'll have some lab reports for you tomorrow, too. Everything else is fine, by the way."

"Fine." Morrison looked at his chest. The eight rubber nipples were stuck on with tape, and wires led from them into a small flat box. He looked at the box.

"You keep it in your pocket," Williams explained.

"I feel bionic."

"When you can't see it, you'll forget that it's there. . . . You can get dressed now." Williams started to leave.

"Charlie?"

"What?"

"My heart. Does it really sound bad?"

"I didn't say it sounded *bad.*"

"You didn't say it sounded good."

"Yeah. Right. I didn't say it sounded good."

The studio was A, the big studio, and for a moment Morrison stood in the doorway looking at the whole musical crowd and hearing the big musical jangle as the brass and the flutes and the strings tuned up and the drummer brushed a tentative *whssh* on the lids.

So this is it, he thought. The ticket away from Hamilton Rush and drain-cleaner crises, good-bye, Mr. Chunky . . . or else it was just another demo session, something he'd been through a thousand times before; only this time there wasn't any creep-head client sitting in the booth and ordering tubas and lyric changes and pastrami on white. This time, whatever he recorded was his, a hundred percent, win or lose, and at least there was some kind of comfort in that.

And there was no piano player.

He stared for a second at the empty bench, and then strode to the control room, heading for Warner, who was sitting at the console with a young engineer. "All *right*," he started, "you welsher, you—"

"Hi," Warner cut him off, smiling nicely. "Bob, this is Kenny. Kenny, Bob."

The engineer smiled; Morrison glowered and turned back to Warner. "OK. Buddy, Where's the piano? We had a deal, and I finished *my* part, God only knows. I'm wired like a freaking undercover cop and—"

"Relax."

"I'm not supposed to relax. I'm supposed to be measured under terrible stress. Charlie said. And you're certainly—"

"Bob shut up and turn around."

Mario stood at the door with Davey.

Morrison stood there staring for a second, then slowly shook his head and started to laugh. "Oh, no," he said, "you're too . . . Oh, man." He went over to Davey and hugged him hard, and then, pulling away, he said, "You creep. You're slumming, right?"

Davey shrugged. "I didn't have anything else to do, so I got on a plane."

"You're supposed to play a concert in Boston tomorrow."

"So? That's tomorrow. This is today." Davey rubbed his hands together and clapped them.

"Okay. Are we jawing around or working? 'Cause one thing I—"

"Get your tail on the bench."

Morrison headed back for the studio, Davey at his side. "I don't know," he said, "if you're right for this job. Can you read music?"

"Just the upper staff."

"Good. I don't write for the left hand anyway." Morrison tapped his finger on the chart. "You come in at C—"

"Robert. Go away. I can read music."

"Right." Morrison went away. Jumpy as a cat, he thought, as a kitten, as a kid, as a Mexican jumping bean, and he fingered the little black box in his pocket. How'm I doin', Charlie? How's this for stress?

"Okay." He took his position in the center, lifted the baton. "Bar twenty-one. That's a tricky tempo change there, and I want . . ." He finished his instructions. They ran through it once. It was the title song, and he wanted to get it down first; it was the hardest, and the most important. After the first run-through, he rubbed his eyes, ran his hands through his hair, and looked up at the control booth.

"How's the balance in there?"

Kenny nodded, and Warner's voice through the speaker said, "Fine."

"Okay." There was still a lot wrong. No, not a lot. Just a little. But a little was a lot. "Okay." He addressed the orchestra now. "We got a sloppy attack, but we know that, right? It's a-one-and-two-and-*WHANG*, okay? Davey? For the hell of it, give me a D diminished on forty instead of what I've got, and everybody, let's pick it up a hair when we bounce back to Go. Okay?"

145

"Hey, Bob," Kenny's voice said. "You want to put this one down, or what?" and Morrison, rubbing his jaw, looked up.

And Jennifer was there. Not in the control booth, but standing right there on the studio floor, just inside the doorway.

"How long have you been here?"

"I think I came in on the 'two-and-*WHANG.*'"

"Oh." He nodded. "Right on cue."

She was wearing a tan silk blouse and chinos and a pink sweater and her hair was . . .

"*Bob?* You want to put it down?"

Morrison looked at the control booth now. "Sure. What the hell. It's only tape." He looked back at Jen. "I didn't expect you."

"I . . . didn't either."

"You're in the wrong room, you know. You're supposed to—"

She flushed. "You want me to go?"

"I want you to stay. Just get thee behind me."

She flushed again. "What does that mean?"

"It means I can't look at you and do anything else at the same time."

"Oh." Again she flushed. And he was really astounded at the clamor of his heart. He briefly considered making liner notes for Charlie. *Zigzag 27: Jennifer flushed.* There was a stool near the piano. She sat on it, saying something to Davey, and Morrison turned.

"Okay," he said, "we're putting this down," and waited till he heard the control-room voice slugging the tape: "Take One. 'If Ever I See You Again.'" There was silence for a second.

He rubbed his jaw, then nodded. "And a-one-and-a-two-and . . ."

It was fine. He could feel it being fine. He could feel himself standing in the middle of Music, and that felt fine, and for a moment, winning or losing didn't matter because, just for a moment, he felt that he'd won, that he'd done something good, something pleasing to himself, and maybe that was all you ever got out of life, and most people probably never got that.

The last vibration of the last note died. "Yeah," he said softly, and looked at the booth. Mario was building him a bull's-eye sign.

"Let's hear it back," Morrison said. "And see if it's the real Ella Fitzgerald."

He turned to Davey. And there was Jen. And it struck him as crazy, impossible, hopeful, that for several seconds he'd forgotten she was there.

"It was beautiful," she said. "It was just . . . beautiful." And then she stood up, slinging her shoulder bag back on her shoulder, and he thought: Oh God, she's doing it again. Hit and Run. And he knew when she was gone he would *not* be able to forget she *wasn't* there.

But he just said, "Oh. I gather you're leaving."

She nodded. "I have to. A dumb appointment at the gallery."

"Oh."

"But I'll see you later," she said.

"Later," he repeated, as though it were a word in Serbo-Croatian. "What does that mean?"

"I thought I was taking you to dinner," she said.

"Oh."

She said, "Unless you've changed your mind."

"No," he said. "One mind-changer is enough in any crowd. I'm booked here till nine."

"Why don't I pick you up back at your hotel?"

"Fine."

"Nine-thirty?"

"Fine."

And she left. Leaving him free to forget she was gone, because he'd see her "later." A really beautiful word, he thought. One of the finest in the whole Serbo-Croatian tongue.

She drove to the gallery, wondering again what she was doing, and not expecting an answer from herself. She was full of surprises today, riddles she couldn't answer. She'd hung up the phone before, after he'd called, after she'd dutifully told him no, and instead of feeling virtuous, placid, relieved, she'd found herself eagerly wishing to scream.

She did not ordinarily relish introspection. If something pained you, you did not sit and sulk; nor did you stand there poking the wound. You went for a swim. Or better still, you painted a picture, and whatever was going on in your mind went out through your fingertips: big, bright lines. You did not have to understand what you painted; you did not have to understand what you felt. If you felt like screaming, then maybe you screamed.

She went out to the beach, and instead of screaming, she stared at the sea, seeing it suddenly in different light. What she'd loved

about the ocean was its parable of freedom—
the limitless horizon, the unruly waves—but it
suddenly occurred to her that freedom was an
illusion, that nothing, and least of all she, was
free. The entire ocean was manned by the
moon, pulled back and forth, daily, like a pull
toy—tide in, tide out—so predictable the tide
times were printed in the paper so fishermen
and sailors could decide when to sail, and the
moon was simply the earth's balloon, held on a
string, and wild animals roamed because they
had to, yanked by an instinct, and swallows
flew to Capistrano on command, and her
very own precious, vaunted freedom was
nothing but a prison cell with a view. Locking
others out, it locked her in. And it suddenly
seemed as unbearable, as dismally ironic as
that.

She'd gone back to the house and, doing no
thinking, she'd dressed hurriedly and left in
the car.

Only now it seemed foolish and confusing
again, or even superstitious. As though she'd
taken action based on a dream.

He waited in the lobby, checking his watch,
and wondered, almost wearily: What now?—
and whether the girl who would meet him
would be warm or chilly or both in turn. It
struck him again that love, instead of the
grandest of human emotions, was probably
the most asinine. Certainly the least realistic.
A passion for football had a sounder basis.
Considering, at least, that he'd spent more
time with the New York Giants than with
Jennifer Corley. One crazy night as a kid.

Followed by a diner breakfast and a brush-off. And thirteen years later, a kiss on a raft. A recitation of the mere Events would lead nobody sane to call it a love story. And yet it was also the classic love story; Leander had swum the Hellespont for less.

When she finally arrived, she was very Bright. They had dinner in a quiet French restaurant, and she was full of Chatter. She told him she'd met at the gallery with a Mr. Compton of Spring Loom Mills who wanted, he told her, to reproduce *Morning #128* on a "'fine arts collection for bedroom and bath.' He *refused* to call them sheets and washcloths," she said. "But he offered me twenty-five thousand dollars and a nickle a pillowcase, or something like that."

"And what did you say?"

She shrugged, smiling. "I suppose I'm stupid. But I kept on picturing terrible people cleaning their ears out with parts of my soul."

"So you told him no."

She nodded.

He laughed. "Integrity," he said.

"You think it's stupid."

"I think it's terrific. Somebody has to keep holding the flame in this dim, dark world."

Flushing, she shrugged again, shaking her head. "I won't win any contests for Honor." She twisted her wineglass around on the table. "I . . . uh . . . shouldn't be here," she said, looking up.

He cocked his head, waiting.

She pushed a strand of yellow hair from her eyes. "I promised someone I wouldn't do this."

"What?"

"This."

"See me?"

"Yes."

He nodded slowly. "Why? Am I a threat?"

She shrugged. "He doesn't even know that I'm here."

"Where is he?"

"On a business trip—out of town."

"And if he were *in* town . . . would you still be here?"

She nodded slowly. "I'm afraid so. Yes."

"Ah! Afraid. *Why* are you afraid? Are you really *afraid?*"

She nodded.

"Why?"

"Because . . . I just don't trust this situation."

He stared at her a moment. "What situation? We're having dinner. People have dinner all the time. This restaurant is *full* of people having dinner. *All* restaurants are full of people having dinner. So what situation?"

"Stop playing games."

"*Games?*" he exploded. "Honey, when it comes to the roster of games, you're the one who's got the Olympic medals. Me, I'm just a fan who curses in the bleachers. So I'm asking you, sincerely, *what* situation?"

"It's dangerous," she said to him flatly. "And you know it."

"*What's* dangerous?" He narrowed his eyes. "I don't pack a gun. I'm not gonna shanghai you off to Topeka. If I'm dumb enough to love you, it's none of your business. It doesn't even have to take any of your time. You can sleep

151

right through it. Listen to me, Jen, what are you afraid of?"

She was very quiet for a very long time. Then she said quietly, "Getting involved."

"Get-ting in-volved." He parced it acidly. "You have gotten so involved in *not* getting involved that getting involved is *simple* in comparison." She almost smiled, but her mind changed her lips. "Getting involved is just letting something happen, you know? Just relaxing." He cocked his head at her. "What about this guy who's . . . uh . . . out of town? Aren't you . . . aren't you involved with *him?*"

She shook her head no, with her eyes on the table, and he noticed the smallest silvering of tears.

"Oh, baby," he said gently, and reached across the table, taking her hand. Gripping it, she looked up, smiling, sniffing, and said, "I'm a mess, you know. I'm really a mess."

He grinned at her slowly. "Yeah. So am I."

"*You're* not a mess. You're . . . connected. You've . . . dealt with the world, just as it is. You haven't run away from it . . . you've kept on trying."

He nodded. "Listen, honey. Anybody who tries as hard as I do not to be a mess, is a mess. Believe me."

And she suddenly smiled at him. "You want to have a messier-than-thou contest?"

"No," he said. "You want to have a gooey dessert?"

"No," she said. "I want you to sing me your song."

"What song?"

"The song I heard the music to before."

"Oh, that song. I don't sing at restaurant tables. It went out of style with Sinatra movies. How's your piano?"

"I don't know," she said gravely. "We could go home and ask it."

They asked it. It said, "I'm a lot out of tune, thank you, but it's me or nothing." So he played her the song, and he started to sing

> *Long lonely highways that stretch out*
> *To nowhere*
> *And I'm never turning for home—*

"You sound like Gene Kelly," she said.
"Shut up. I'm performing."
And he got as far as

> *Warm sleepy mornings, waking up*
> *Next to you*

And then she was sitting next to him on the piano bench, and his hands weren't on the keys anymore, and his mouth was saying, "Oh, Jen Jen Jen . . ."

Which wasn't part of the lyric at all.

He carried her into the bedroom, and she was soft in his arms and she said, "My heart's really pounding," and she laughed, "like a drum-da-da-dum. C'mere. I want to feel if yours is, too," and he started to laugh.

And then he remembered the Contraption on his chest. And the wires. Like a sci-fi Terminal Man. And he said, "Just . . . don't start without me, okay?" and he raced to the bathroom and ripped the things off, painfully, tearing out hair from his chest, and he stashed them, along with the flat black box, in an open cabinet under the sink, and then covered the evidence up with a towel.

"Sorry, Charlie," he said to the towel. "Star-Kist says it's in bad taste."

XIII

When he woke, to the sound of some yelp-
ing gulls, he was surprised to discover she was
still there. She had not been part of a dream.
She had not disappeared into Brigadoon's
mists. She was lying next to him, curving
into him; he could smell the lemon scent of
her hair and feel the tickle of her breath on
his chest. One of his arms was under her back
and one of her arms was thrown across his
waist, and he lay there, quietly marveling at
her, the particular sleeping smile on her face,
the particular way her back was arched, the
intricate pattern of her hair on the pillow. He
wanted to move, but he didn't want his move-
ment to make her move. As though the exact
position she was in was a precious and perfect
kaleidoscope picture that, once shattered, would
never come again.

He wondered now how he'd lived without her, how he'd ever been able to wake in the morning, or sleep at night, or scrounge meaning out of dry days, and she stirred suddenly, moving in his arms, scratching her head and, eyes still closed, she murmered, "Time is it?"

"Early," he said, looking at the clock. "Quarter of six."

"Too early," she said. "Sleep," she said, and grinning, kissing the top of her head, rearranging his arm, pulling her closer, Morrison quickly, obediently slept.

He woke into white, dazzling sunlight and blinked, not remembering where he was. And then she slowly came into focus, standing by the window, in a long yellow terry-cloth robe, and he found himself almost afraid for a moment, that when she turned to face him, her eyes would be empty and matter-of-fact. But, turning, her expression was tender, flushed, and he watched with absurd and ridiculous delight as she pivoted quickly, moving toward the bed.

"Get up," she commanded.

Morrison yawned. "I never get up." He yawned again. "It's a bad habit, and once you start, it's impossible to break."

"It's noon," she said, sitting down on the bed and trying to pull the covers away. "Get up."

"It's also bad for your health." Morrison reached for his first cigarette. "Recent statistics have clearly shown that ten out of ten highway accidents happen to people who got out of bed."

"Get up." She laughed and tickled his chest,

and he grabbed her arm. "The sun is shining. We can go for a swim."

"Got a better idea."

"Mmm-hmmm," she said.

"Mmm-hmmm," he said, and he reached for her, tugging the yellow robe, pulling her close for a toothpaste kiss and grunting as his body woke, waking her, feeling her arching into his mood. She moved into his arms as though she'd been there a million times before, and when they finally met, it seemed as though the final piece of a puzzle had somehow miraculously clicked into place.

"I am very happy," she said slowly, and cupped his hand while he lit a cigarette. "I am quite outrageously, impossibly happy."

"I know," he said.

"You know?"

"Mmm-hmmm."

Breakfast on the sunporch. It was one-thirty. She said, "I know where we can get a boat. You want to go sailing?"

He smiled. "Do you?"

She nodded.

"Then I want to go sailing," he said.

He did not ask whose boat it was. It was a fine sailboat, and she seemed surprised that he knew how to handle it.

"I lived on a lake once," he said.

"When you were married?"

"Yes. I'm getting sunburned. Will you pass me the lotion?"

She lotioned his back, and he oiled her shoulders and the back of her legs; his hands memorized them.

He slept again briefly.

"You must be exhausted," she said, waking him. Cold beer and a plate of cold chicken had somehow materialized in her hand.

"And hungry," he said, grabbing for a leg, which did not happen to belong to the chicken.

"Were you in love with your wife?" she asked him later.

He squinted at her through shimmering sun. "At the end, no. In the middle, I don't think so."

"At the beginning?"

"I'm not sure." He was checking the sails. "It had something to do with timing, I guess, and the fact that she loved me, or said she did." He shrugged. "I guess when somebody's never been loved, they'll buy almost anything that's wearing the label."

She thought about that, lying on the deck with her head in his lap. She looked up at him. "What about loving?" she said.

"Yeah, what about it?"

"When you've never loved, how do you know what you're feeling is love?"

He thought about that, stroking her hair. "When you're in love," he said, "your toes turn purple and your thumbnails break."

"Oh," she said, looking at her broken nails and the spot of purple paint on her toe.

At the dock they bought double-decker ice-cream cones.

"Vanilla," he said. "You're actually, truly *choosing* vanilla?"

"It's the only flavor that doesn't have artificial flavors and dyes."

"Safe ice cream." He shook his head. "The woman even chooses safe ice cream."

"All right," she said, "swap me a scoop of yours." He fed her a scoop of his chocolate-chip mint.

"You know what happens," she announced gravely, "from eating ice cream with artificial dyes?"

"What?"

"The tip of your nose turns green." And she licked the ice cream off the tip of his nose.

They walked from the marina back to the house, on sun-hot sand, with an ocean breeze chilling the air.

"When are you going back?" she said.

"Mmm. What's today?"

"Friday."

"Then I guess I'm leaving tomorrow," and he added lightly, laughing when he said it, "which'll just give you time to pack a few bags and cancel the milkman."

She said nothing. They walked down the beach.

After a while she said, "Must it be tomorrow?"

He nodded. "Sunday's my kid's birthday. I told him I'd take him to a Knicks game."

"Oh."

He kicked up some sand. "No way I can stay. He's seven, you know? And he doesn't even remember his mother. And he's counting on me, Jen. But I'm not just bucking to be Daddy of the Year. I adore that kid. He's wonderful." He looked at her. "You'd love him, too."

She said nothing.

A wooden boardwalk led to her house. They climbed to the boardwalk.

"Bob?" she said, and he knew he didn't want to hear the rest of that sentence. "Don't—"

"Don't" he cut her off. "Just don't say it. Whatever you were going to say, just take a deep breath and swallow it."

"I can't," she said. "It's got to be said."

He said nothing. The boardwalk was hot. He felt a splinter go into his toe. He kept walking.

"Where do you think we're going?" she said.

"To your house."

"You're not thinking," she said.

"And you're thinking too much. I know that without even hearing what you're thinking."

"I've been thinking about us," she said. "All day."

"Yeah. So have I."

"No," she said. "You've been dreaming about us. *I've* been thinking." She was looking at the ocean. "There's no place we can go."

"There's no place we *can't* go. It just started."

She turned to him, her eyes as blue as the sea. "Would you want me to go to New York?" she said. "Because my work's out here. And I hate New York. And according to rumor, you hate California."

He nodded. "And even if I didn't," he said, "I got a big bad business to run in New York. If I don't get this picture, I've got to run it. And I hate California. I don't understand it." He stopped walking. "But I love *you*, so I guess I could try . . ." But she lowered her eyes, shaking her head, and he said, "And I don't understand you, either."

She started to move again.

"We'll work something out," he said. "We'll work something out."

They were climbing her stairs. She was shaking her head. "There's my work," she said. "I've got my work. Even if you came out here, hating the place, I can't be a painter and a wife and a mother."

"Did I ask you to marry me?"

"No. But you would."

He nodded. "I would." They were standing at her door. "But I wouldn't want you to give up painting. I wouldn't expect you to cook and clean. Look, could you just come to New York for a—"

"No!" Her tone seemed to startle her too. "No," she said softly. "When I work, I can work for twenty straight hours."

"Hell, so can I. We could meet for lunch every second Thursday in the linen closet. Jen, I don't—"

"Don't," she cut him off. "Please don't. Please don't ask me for things I can't give. I'm trying—"

"You're *very* trying," he snapped.

She stared at him. "I'll drive you back to your hotel."

"I'll take a taxi."

"Don't be silly," she said.

They drove in silence. Jennifer turned the radio on. And the Jungle jingle blasted the air. He snapped it off. They drove in silence.

At the front of his hotel, she pulled to the

curb, and when he reached for the door handle, she said, "Wait."

"For what?" He turned.

She looked at him. "I . . . I'm sorry," she said. "I knew how this would end and I shouldn't have started it.

He sighed. "You're always sorry for the wrong things. You ought to be sorry you're ending it, Jen. I said that I didn't understand you before. I do. I understand you're protecting yourself. And you're *protecting* yourself right out of living. Jennifer, stop playing Sleeping Beauty. Wake up and grab it before it's too late."

But all she did was sit there shaking her head.

"You'll wake up one day and regret it," he said. He smiled. "And I wish I could say 'I won't be there.' But I will." He opened the door, stepped out to the curb.

"Good-bye," she said.

"Good night," he said. "Pleasant dreams."

Coda

XIV

New York was dressed for Christmas again. Department stores sprouted tinsel stalactites, radios blared "only ten days more," street corners rang with the jingle of bells, and somber Salvation Army trombonists killed any chances of "Peace on Earth."

Morrison went Christmas shopping. He bought Elsa a black snakeskin bag. He bought Warner a T-shirt that said SOLD OUT, he bought Mario, who claimed to be going on a diet, a life-size silver-plated Hershey bar from Tiffany's, and while he was there, he passed by a counter and noticed a silver heart on display. The same silver necklace that Jennifer was wearing that first afternoon. He stopped and stared at it.

"Sir? Can I help you?"

"No," he said dryly. "I'm beyond help."

He walked up the avenue to FAO Shwarz, the world's most sublime and extravagant toy store, whose initials, he'd once told Johnathan gravely, actually meant "For Adults Only." He spent several hours looking at toys, carefully choosing an electric train. It was wonderful. A long, seven-car train on a figure-eight track, and of course he had to buy the surrounding scenery, the trees and mountains, the overhead bridge, and the railroad station and a tiny conductor, and the signal lights, and a couple of houses, and while he was at it, a giant Victorian dollhouse for Amy.

At four, though he was still supposed to be on vacation, he stopped at the office. "What ho-ho-hoes," Warner asked, looking up.

Morrison built an electric smile. "The best electric train in the world. When I was a kid, I'd've killed for that train."

"Where is it?" Warner said.

"I'm having it sent." Morrison laughed. "I guess we can't play with it till after Christmas. Or better—come over on Christmas day."

"Yeah? Will Johnathan let us near it?"

"Don't worry. I'll send him to bed without supper." Morrison laughed.

"Ho-ho-ho," Warner said flatly.

Morrison grimaced. "What's that supposed to mean?"

"It means I hear the echo of hollow laughter, of made-up merriment and manic depression."

"Oh. That," Morrison said, pacing over to the filing cabinet, glancing at the window, and pacing back. "Forget it. This too—as someone or other once said—will pass." He slid to a chair and lifted his shoulders. "In about a hundred and eight million years."

"Nice," Warner said. "Nice little jobby you're doing on yourself. Listen. Look. Will you believe me, Bob? It worked out for the best. The lady's a loser."

"Right. She lost me."

"Let's hear that again with a little conviction."

"Maybe next year."

"Speaking of which, we're having a giant New Year's blast."

"Wake me when it's over."

"I want you to come. Barbara wants you to come. She wants you to come with Caroline Walters, to be exact."

"Oh, look. Don't try to fix me up, huh? I'm not completely backward. I can get my own dates." Morrison took a cigarette from his pocket and glanced at the work chart up on the wall. "How's business?"

"Terrific. Never been better. Only, everyone's waiting for *you* to get back."

"Yeah? And when am I officially back?"

"Well, I've been telling them the first of the year. You should have your answer from Hollywood by then. If it's yes, I'm a liar. If it's no, I figure you'll take the kids away on vacation and come back simply champing to work."

"I'd like to work now. I think it would get my mind off things."

"You want to write a theme song for Kitchen Tune-Up?"

"What?"

"It's the new drain unclogger. 'Puts your kitchen drain in tune.'"

Morrison nodded. "'Singin' in the Drain.'"

Warner shook his head. "By George, he's got it. I'm not even kidding. I think that's great."

"Yeah. I've an absolute genius for stupidity." Morrison stood. "You want me to write it?"

"You want to?"

"No. But I think I will." He yawned. "Business as usual, right?"

"Right."

"I think I'll write it at home." He started for the door. "By the way"—he turned—"Davey's on Channel Thirteen tomorrow night."

"I know. They taped his Boston concert. Laura invited us over to watch."

"Yeah. I was thinking," Morrison said. "Their set's about ninety-seven years old. Black and white, and haunted with ghosts. Would they hate it if I bought them a color portable? I mean for Christmas, but in time for tomorrow?"

"No. They'd love it."

"Good. Then I will." Morrison shrugged. "If Hollywood calls me, I'll be at Korvette's."

"Is that a tree, or is that a tree?" Morrison asked, standing on top of the kitchen ladder, looping the final light on a branch.

"That is a tree," Amy agreed.

"Or else it's a tree," Johnathan said.

And Morrison laughed, folding the stool. At least, he thought, I've given them that. A sense of humor; a sense of play. Moving back from the decorated tree, a few strands of tinsel sticking to his sweater, he said, "Oh-oh-oh. We forgot the angel."

Amy said, "No we didn't. It's here." She produced the angel for the top of the tree. "Can I put it up?"

"It's my turn, my turn," Johnathan complained. "Last year Amy got to put it on top and you said that *next* year—"

"You just made that up," Morrison said.

"I don't think so," Johnathan said. "I remember."

"All right. Okay. You do it this year, and next year, Amy—"

"That's what happened *last* year," Johnathan said. "Only in reverse."

"Okay. Here's the angel."

"Lift me."

"C'mon." Morrison scooped him up by the waist; he was holding him high when the knife-pain started to cut through his chest. "You done?" he said slowly through gritted teeth.

"Got it," Johnathan said.

"Okay."

Morrison put him down on the floor and walked to the sofa, sweating slightly.

"Daddy?"

"Sssh. Get me a glass of water, will you?"

"Daddy?"

"Get it!"

Both the kids went, looking confused, and by the time they came back, the pain had subsided. He lit a cigarette in celebration, because it was tension, that's all it was, and he suddenly remembered the wired nipples he'd left in the towel under Jennifer's sink.

He wondered what she'd made of it.

". . . want your water?" Amy was saying.

"Sure I want it." Morrison drank. "I think it's bedtime," he said when he'd finished.

Amy said, "Creeps. It's not even eight."

"Yeah. But it's *my* bedtime," he said.

"Would you read us a story before you go to bed? And then we'll tuck you in." Johnathan giggled.

"Sure. A story," Morrison said. "Okay. What story would you like to hear? 'Snow White and the Seven Santinis'? or 'Rudolph, the Red-Nosed Doppelgänger'? Huh?"

Johnathan laughed. Amy said she wanted a grown-up story, but Johnathan wanted a Christmas story.

He thought. "A grown-up Christmas story." He walked to the bookshelf, rubbing his jaw. "There aren't any grown-up Christmas stories," but then he saw the worn O. Henry collection, and after the children were pajamaed and scrubbed, he sat down and read them "The Gift of the Magi."

"I don't *get* it," Amy said. "I think that's dumb. *She* cut off all of her beautiful hair to buy him a chain for his favorite watch, only *he* hocked his watch to buy her the combs. That's dumb."

"That's love," Morrison said.

"Well then, *love* is dumb," Amy concluded, from a lotus position on the upper bunk. "And it's also impractical," she added, yawning.

"Oh, I am spawning a cynical brat."

She looked at him sleepily, pursing her lips. "What's 'cynical'?" she said.

"Well . . . it's being so smart it's a sin." Morrison frowned at her, shaking his head. "Don't be like that, Amy. Promise you won't."

170

She tilted her head at him. "Okay," she said. "Will you take me skating tomorrow again?"

"Sure. You want to go to Central Park?"

"Uh-huh."

"Okay. Right after school. I have to do a little more shopping first."

"Yeah? For us?" Johnathan said.

"Nope. I already got your presents. A huge bowl of spinach and a nice umbrella. Tomorrow I'm shopping for Davey and Laura, and I wish that Christmas didn't make you crass. Christmas, Crassmas," Morrison said.

"Christmas, Crassmas," Johnathan repeated, yawning.

"Daddy?" Amy said.

"What?"

"I was thinking."

"What?"

"I'd cut my hair off for *you*."

Morrison laughed. "That's dumb," he said.

The saleswoman said, "I'm very sorry. But we certainly can't deliver by *tonight*. We aren't even promising delivery by Christmas."

Morrison looked at the television set.

"Uh-huh. All right. Then I'll take it with me."

"It's heavy," she said. "Fifty-one pounds."

He glared at her. "Right. I'll take it with me."

He wrote out the check, wondering why everyone thought he was a weakling. The stock boy came out with the large carton, tied with a cord.

It wasn't that heavy.

He was only very slightly winded when he got the taxi, and the driver waited, rather impatiently, while Morrison hoisted the carton to the seat, and then gave him Davey's West Side address.

He checked his watch. 12:42. He could pick up Amy at 2:30 and still have time for a burger at Stark's.

The carton seemed heavier the second time out, and by the time he'd made it to the top of the stoop, he was already starting to hear himself rasp.

In the outside hallway, he punched the buzzer for apartment 7, and Laura answered.

"Ah," she said, "coming to scrounge another lunch from us, eh?"

"Uh-uh," he said. "I got a little Christmas present for the kids, and I thought you might let me hide it in your closet," and he heard her say to Davey, "It's your crazy friend Bob. He just bought a Christmas present for our closet," and she hung up, buzzing the noisy buzzer that opened the door to the downstairs hall.

He kicked the carton to the edge of the stairway, and, giving himself a countdown of three, hoisted it quickly up by the cord.

On the third-floor landing, he stopped for a rest and his heart was booming like a thousand cannons and his mother's voice wailed at him, "Bobby, Bobby, what are you *doing*? You *know* you're not supposed to play basketball yet," and cursing, he lifted the box to his shoulders and started to walk up the final flight.

The pain attacked him like an angry mugger. Obscenely, swiftly, it pushed him downstairs.

Reprise

XV

The snow—a predicted seventeen inches, predicted to start the day before Christmas, predicted to paralyze Kennedy Airport, predicted to mess up everyone's plans—held itself off until Christmas morning, and the final airplane that landed, at noon, landed on a runway ribboned with white.

At the air-freight office, under a sign that said SHIP IT EARLY, the clerks were handling last-minute packages, shipped at exorbitant premium rates, and messengers stood by, ready to deliver them, also at exorbitant premium rates.

One of the clerks grabbed a large package, a flat box, about three by four, marked, "Fragile, Artwork, Handle with Care," and checked out the package against his list. The list had a note saying, "Do Not Deliver." Frowning slightly, he scratched his jaw and said to his partner, "Hey, Reamer. This one says 'Do Not Deliver.' "

"So?" Reamer looked up at him.

"So? Why do you suppose they don't want it delivered?"

"*I* don't know why," Reamer snapped. "And I really got enough to be worrying about with the packages everyone *does* want delivered. Maybe the sender doesn't want him to have it. Maybe he doesn't want it. Maybe he's dead. How the hell do *I* know."

The first clerk shrugged. "You don't have to get so nasty about it. I was just asking."

"Don't ask," Reamer muttered. "Just work. Don't ask."

Laura turned her head from the car window and looked at Warner, who was sitting beside her, holding a funeral wreath on his lap. The wreath was large, made of white gladioli, and the black satin ribbon that girded the thing said "Many Happy Returns of the Day."

"You're disgusting," she said. "It isn't funny."

"He would have liked it," Warner said grimly. "You know what a sense of humor he had."

Mario was carrying a large box wrapped in a cheerful red-and-green paper and tied with a violent turquoise ribbon.

"Is that for the children?" Elsa said at the door.

"For one of them," Mario said. "Where is he?"

"If you mean the big one," Elsa muttered, "he's whirling around in his baseball mitt."

"How's he feeling?" Mario said, putting down the package and shucking his coat.

"Frighteningly well," Elsa sighed. "He keeps on saying it was the mildest heart attack in the history of the human heart." Sighing again, she took Mario's coat. "I half-wish they'd kept him in the hospital longer. I'm just afraid he'll start overdoing again."

"He's really okay," Mario assured her. "We spoke to the doctor. He's really okay." He followed her into the living room now, placing the package under the tree. "In fact, the doctor told us it was probably lucky. The attack, I mean. Like a warning, you know. If he hadn't had a mild one to scare him to death, he might've had a big one that—"

"Mario, Mario," Amy yelled, coming into the room in a velvet dress. "Do you like my dress, we're having a turkey, did you bring Roger?"

Mario laughed. "I like your dress, I know we're having turkey, and Roger's with his mother. She's parking the car."

"How come Rosalind's parking the car?"

"It's my Christmas present," Mario said, and when the doorbell rang, he hollered, "I'll get it," and went to the door.

Davey, Laura, Warner, and Barbara entered with packages, stamping their snowy boots on the mat.

Amy looked at the black-and-white wreath. "That's ugly," she said.

Warner grinned. "Isn't it? I thought it was atrocious myself." He looked at his wife. "Where shall I put it?"

"Right in the garbage can," Barbara said flatly.

"Around his neck," Davey suggested.

"Around whose neck?" Morrison said. He stood by the tree, holding Johnathan's hand.

"Consider it a giant ring around the collar," Warner said, tossing the wreath on the couch. "Welcome home, jerk-o," he added dryly.

"Don't call my daddy names," Amy said angrily, running into Morrison's arms. And he smiled at her, holding her close for a moment. "She's a dumb broad," he said, "but exceedingly loyal. . . . You guys want a drink?"

Laura said, "Why don't you go and sit down. We'll fix our own drinks."

"I don't want to sit down," Morrison said, but he sat on the sofa, next to the wreath. "In fact, I'm supposed to exercise a lot. 'A balanced program of exercise and rest.' Sounds like a commercial for something."

"For life," Laura said. She and Barbara were arranging packages under the tree. "And I really hope you learned a lesson," she added.

"Right on, I did."

Morrison sighed. "Lying in that hospital bed for a week, I really learned something vitally important."

"What did you learn?" Davey said flatly.

"Why Santa Claus comes down the chimney, man." Morrison laughed.

No one else did.

"Can we open the presents?" Johnathan said.

"Will you take it seriously?" Mario said. "Will you seriously take it seriously, Bob?"

Morrison nodded, looking at his children. "Yeah," he said.

There was silence for a moment.

"Can we open the presents?" Johnathan said, and the doorbell rang. It was Rosalind, Roger, and Janie Marino, and Amy was suddenly staring quite closely at Morrison's knee, because Amy had a crush on Roger Marino, and the bell rang again, and Elsa went running, and Warner's mother and father came in, with their grandchildren, Bobby, David, and Nell.

Bobby said, *"We* couldn't find a place to park, and *Daddy* parked in front of a fire hydrant, and *Grampa* says Daddy's gonna really be sorry," and Barbara said, "Your Daddy's a reckless parker."

"Can we open the *presents?"* Johnathan said.

They opened the presents. Squeals from the children. Morrison put on a record of carols. "And now it's time for the grown-up presents," Mario said. "Here's one for you, Bob," and handed him the box with the turquoise ribbon. "It's just what you wanted."

"One cigarette," Morrison said. "All I want for Christmas is one cigarette. Hasn't anyone noticed I quit? Cold turkey."

"If you didn't quit, you'd *be* a cold turkey," Warner said. "Open the box."

"Will you open the *box?"* Mario said.

Morrison shrugged and opened the box.

Neatly surrounded by tissue paper was a jumbled collection of bottles and cans: Jungle perfume, Kitchen Tune-Up, Mr. Chunky, Diet-Delish...

"What is this," Morrison growled, "a retrospective of my misspent youth?"

"Will you read the card?" Mario prompted.
"Where is it?"

"Fish," Warner said.

Hidden in the bottom of the box was the card.

> If you ever regret you're in
> the movie business
> Remember the alternative.

Morrison stared at the card and looked up. "What does this mean?" he said suspiciously.

"What do you mean, what does it mean? It means you won the contest," Mario said. "You're scoring the movie."

"I'm scoring the movie?"

"Soznick called. He said he thought you'd written some major hits. The most moving songs in the entire history of moving pictures. He says you can do the work anyway you want to, anywhere you want to, he won't change a word or a note or a flute, but the only thing he said is, don't work too hard." Warner looked up. "Or, to quote him exactly, 'Tell him I'll kill him if he kills himself right. And, by the way, Shirley and LaVerne send their love."

"I always wanted to be loved by a duck."

"That's all you're gonna say?"

"It's not a bad present," Morrison said.

"What's *wrong* with you?" Mario sputtered. "Why don't I see you jumping up and down? You've got absolutely everything you wanted now, right?"

"Yeah. Right." Morrison nodded, and the doorbell rang, and Elsa yelled, "Don't get up. I'll get it, and dinner'll be ready in forty-five minutes."

"Right," Morrison said again slowly, "and only a greedy pig could want more."

"Are you expecting a painting?" Elsa yelled from the doorway.

Morrison looked at her. "Yeah," he said. "To be sent air freight. Is it here?"

She nodded. "You've got to sign for it."

"Oh," he said, getting up from the floor. He looked at Warner. "It's a good painting."

Warner just smiled. "How would you know? You don't know about art, you just know what you love."

Morrison grabbed a pencil from the desk and started for the hallway. "Listen," he said, "it's a beautiful painting. I'd like it even if Picasso did it."

And everyone laughed.

She stood in the hallway, leaning on the door, feeling weak in the knees, and merry and giddy, and wanting to laugh, and hearing the laughter, and wanting to cry, because she might have missed it, might have serenely let it go by, have let all the years go serenely by, like an orderly parade (no drunken drummers in foolish hats, no clumsy cartwheels and orange banners), and what if she'd already let it go by? what if she'd already waited too long? He'd said, "You'll wake up one day and regret it. And I wish I could say 'I won't be there.' But I will." Only, Charlie had called, Charlie Williams, to ask if she'd found any "wired-up gizmos," and then he'd explained to her what they were for, and what had happened on Davey's stairway, and thousands of alarm clocks had started to ring, because *what if he really wouldn't be there, what if he'd never be there again?* and she suddenly saw it: that life didn't wait, that the days went by if you used them or not, and there wasn't much time left for being afraid, only now she was afraid that he wouldn't want her, that he'd look at her calmly, with friendly eyes . . .

He walked through the archway and suddenly stopped, holding his breath, feeling his heart start pounding again, only this time he wasn't afraid of the sound, and he knew exactly why his breath was short, and he simply moved to her, took her in his arms, held her very close, and kissed her very hard, till Mario yelled, "What's going on? How long does it take a man to sign his name?" and Warner said, "I bet he forgot how to spell it," and, laughing, Jennifer pulled away.

"Hello." She smiled.

"Good morning," he said.

DON'T MISS
THESE CURRENT
Bantam Bestsellers

RELAX!
SIT DOWN
and Catch Up On Your Reading!

WE DELIVER!
And So Do These Bestsellers.

Bantam Book Catalog

Here's your up-to-the-minute listing of every book currently available from Bantam.

This easy-to-use catalog is divided into categories and contains over 1400 titles by your favorite authors.

So don't delay—take advantage of this special opportunity to increase your reading pleasure.

Just send us your name and address and 25¢ (to help defray postage and handling costs).